A Matter of Trust

By S J Crabb

Also By S J Crabb

The Diary Of Madison Brown

Premier Deception

The One That Got Away
(Part 1 of The Hardcastle Saga)

Payback
(Part 3 of The Hardcastle Saga)

Copyrighted Material

Copyright © S J Crabb 2016
S J Crabb has asserted her rights under the Copyright, Designs and Patents Act 1988 to be identified as the Author of this work.

This book is a work of fiction and except in the case of historical fact, any resemblance to actual persons, living or dead, is purely coincidental.
This book contains Adult content and is not suitable for ages under 18.

For my family and friends who Support me in everything I do.
Thank you x

Prologue

Nathan was angry. He couldn't believe that she had chosen Ben Hardcastle over him. He had worked so hard finding out all he could on him and still she had chosen him. The sight of her walking back to him and taking his hand played on his mind.

He needed her, more than she would ever realise. He had been a fool messing around with Melissa. His lust for her had overtaken his common sense and now he was paying a heavy price.

He slammed his fist down on to the desk in frustration. This couldn't be the end; he had to find a way to win her back. His mind starts whirring and he taps his finger rhythmically on the desk. As he looks at his computer he gains a small amount of satisfaction at the thought of the mess he left behind. It would take them some time to figure out the mess he left at the stores. Life was certainly not going to be easy for them for quite a while.

He needed a plan to deal with his problem. It may take him longer than he had first thought but he was determined to win, he had to win there was no other choice.

An e mail flashes up from his best friend Bradley. Reading it his heart sinks at the content. He would have to explain to Bradley that he had failed. Bradley was doing well for himself and was keen for Nathan to follow him. In giving up his job at Kinghams, Nathan had taken a huge risk. He couldn't work there any longer though, that much was obvious. He would have to take the job with the company that Bradley works for. It wasn't ideal and it would mean that he would have no contact with Bella. However after last night's confrontation he was sure that Ben would keep her as far away from him now as was possible.

Nathan's mind continued to work hard, thinking of various possibilities and potential avenues to follow. He knew that he would need to dig deeper. It was difficult to find out anything other than rumour about Ben Hardcastle, but he knew that what he needed was there, it may just take longer for him to find.

He had underestimated him and the power that he now held over Bella. I won't make that mistake again he thought grimly. Next time I will be ready and she will have no choice but to come back to me, this isn't over.

Chapter 1

I wake up in Ben's arms and breathe a huge sigh of relief. He is draped over me as usual, his leg and arm pinning me to the bed. I smile to myself, I am safe, it feels like I am home and nothing can touch me. I think back to the wedding that was two days ago. I had chosen Ben over Nathan much to everyone's surprise and dismay. Ben was not liked, that much was evident. He has quite a reputation that follows him around, whereas what was not to like about Nathan? But I know better. Ben is not the monster that he was made out to be, I know that. I had no choice but to choose him, the thought of life without him is unbearable. My thoughts turn to Phoebe and Boris, my friends whose wedding day it was and I feel sorry that Nathan had caused such a scene. It hadn't spoilt it though and they had had a fabulous time. It had been a bit awkward the next day though. I knew that everybody was surprised at my choice and given the things that Nathan had said about Ben it would be some time before they would be able to relax around him.
We had left early the next day for home. I haven't spoken to anyone since and Ben and I have just enjoyed being at home together. Ben had been angry though. In fact I had never seen him so angry and he had spent some time that evening on his phone trying to gauge the damage that Nathan had caused at the stores.

We are back to work today and I am not looking forward to facing everyone. I feel Ben stir and snuggle into him, grateful for just a few more minutes of comfort. His arm tightens over me and I laugh to myself as I feel his reaction to me. Once again excitement rushes through me at the thought of what I know will come next. I can feel him gently kissing the back of my neck and his fingers moving expertly over my body. I pretend not to notice and pretend to still be asleep but my body as usual gives me away. I will always try to play games with him but I always lose in the end. His hold is too powerful over me. Arching back into him I know that he is now aware that I am awake. He pulls me around to face him and I can see the love mixed with desire in his face. He doesn't speak and kisses me so passionately and deeply that my insides turn to liquid desire. He always has this effect on me and I am always ready for him. He moves inside me and gently rocks against me.

It is a slow and sensual movement and the feeling of him deep within me drives me to an early climax. He holds me against him as the waves crash over me and he then says, "Morning Bella, did you sleep well?" I laugh as he sounds so matter of fact. He knows the effect that he has on me and plays it to his advantage all the time.

I pull back from him and kiss him gently. "Morning Ben that was a rude awakening." He laughs and grabs my bottom, pinching it hard. "Sorry, I would have taken longer but we have jobs to go to. You won't get away so lightly later though. I want you here in this bed by 7.30pm ready for me and you won't leave it until I have well and truly had my wicked way with you." I push him and jump out of bed. "Always in control hey Ben. Well you may have met your match in me; I may decide to catch up with friends instead." He winks at me and we both know that I will be here waiting for him. I pretend to put up a fight but as it is all I want too we know that it is just a charade.

Ben drops me off at Kinghams and is then heading off to the Head office. He has driven out of his way but wouldn't let me make my own way there. As we pull up he looks at me with concern. "Will you be ok? If you get any problems let me know immediately." I smile trying to reassure him but I know that he can see through my bravado. This is not going to be easy. Everyone will have read the email that Nathan sent to all of the staff, telling them of Ben and I's involvement. Being the boss of several department stores, Kingham's included won't make me popular with my fellow co workers.

The fact that Nathan was also well liked and has been supposedly pushed out of a job also won't sit well. With a deep breath I head through the staff entrance. Mick from security nods at me and then looks away nervously. My heart sinks as he always used to offer me a cheery hello. I make my way to my office and notice that anyone I see on the way looks the other way. I know that it is on purpose, I can sense the atmosphere already. Reaching my office I push open the door and sit down at my desk. I am the first one in so turn on my computer to read the e mail for myself in private.

Well Nathan certainly hasn't pulled any punches. The email is a damning account of our break up, blaming Ben for taking me away and threatening him with losing his job. He also explains that he had no choice but to leave and couldn't do so without letting everybody know how he was threatened and forced out.

Sinking back into my chair I feel a huge weight descend upon me. I would be the one to suffer for this, not Ben. He would be in his ivory tower, nobody would challenge him or make him feel bad, and after all he was still their boss. No, I would be the one to face the brunt of this and there would be no escaping it. Even if I transferred to another store it wouldn't matter. The email went to every member of staff in the Hardcastle group. The damage has been well and truly done.

As I sit there contemplating it all the door opens and April breezes in. "Hi Bella, good weekend?" she says cheerily. My heart sinks as she obviously hasn't read the email. I wonder if she will be quite so friendly once she has read it. I smile thinly at her and she notices my expression and frowns in concern. "What is it Bella, can you tell me?" I nod and say, "You will soon know when you read Nathan's all staff email. Read it first and then I will explain." Looking mystified she turns on her computer and before long I watch her reading the email.

I can see the shock on her face and my heart nose dives. Spinning around she looks at me, her expression a mixture of shock and horror. Pushing back her chair she races over to me and to my surprise envelops me in the biggest hug that she has ever given me. "Oh Bella, I am sorry. This e mail is hideous. You must be so upset." Surprised I pull away and say, "Don't you hate me April? I thought that you would, it appears that everyone else that has read it does." Shaking her head she says, "Of course I don't hate you. I know the story behind this email that Nathan has conveniently missed out. He was to blame for losing you and so what if you have found happiness with Ben. Good on you both."

Feeling a bit happier I say, "But what about the fact that he says that he was forced to quit?" She looks at me grimly and says, "Well I don't believe that for a minute. There are laws to protect him you know and he could have stayed if he really wanted to. He has probably got a great new job and is using that to stick the knife in. Don't worry I will soon put everyone straight." I feel relieved. At least one person doesn't hate me. I smile gratefully at her and she laughs and says, "I never liked Nathan anyway." We both laugh as we know that she loved Nathan. However I understand that she is going to back me up fully and I love her for it. Her phone rings and she turns to answer it. I get on with my work and try to concentrate.

As the day goes on it soon becomes apparent that something has gone dreadfully wrong. The tills are all over the place and the prices that come up are way below what the products should be. Soon the decision is made to shut down the system and enter everything manually. This will mean that the information will be wrong to re order what is sold and I recognise that this is a serious problem. I don't call Ben as I realise that he will be flat out trying to sort out the problem. With a sinking feeling I put two and two together and realise that this is Nathan's parting gift. I can only hope that it is the only one but I know that deep down there is more to come. The atmosphere around the store is tense. Nobody will look at me and anyone that has to ask me anything or talk to me does so in a cold and unfriendly manner.

April does her best but even she can't protect me from the looks and actions of the hostile staff. All in all it is a terrible day and I can't wait for it to end.

I do get a text from Ben asking if I am ok and to call him if I need to. I won't though because I know that he has more pressing matters to deal with.

By the end of the day I can't get out of there fast enough. I get a cab back to Ben's house. Even though I am officially moving in next week it still feels strange to call it home. He e mailed to say that he would be late and to make my own way back. I pick up some groceries before getting the cab so that I can at least make him a nice dinner, as he will be stressed and tired after this trying day.

Thinking about the day's events a feeling of dread begins to form in my stomach. I know that this is all just the beginning. Feeling unnerved I wait for Ben to come home.

Chapter 2

I make us a chicken casserole and wait for him to come home. He finally arrives at 8pm and rushes in looking totally stressed out. Rushing up to him I give him a big hug, holding onto him tightly. He pulls back and smiles ruefully at me. "That's the best welcome I could have after the day I've had," he says and then kisses me gently.
Pulling back he says, "I'm sorry, I distinctly remember that we had other plans for this evening."
Laughing at him I say, "They can wait. You need to eat first and I will pour you a large glass of wine to help you forget about your awful day. Whilst I'm doing that go and get changed and I'll dish up." Still holding on tightly to me he smiles gently and says, "I could get used to having you look after me." "Well you had better get used to it because I fully intend to do just that," I say softly and then push him away. "Come on hurry up, you must be starving."
He winks and then heads off to get changed. I dish up our food and pour us both a large glass of wine each. Over dinner he tells me about his nightmare day. Listening to him speak he tells me that every store was affected. The sales were considerably down because of it and there was chaos as a result. They had called in the epos system engineers who will be working through the night to resolve it. I can tell that he is

worried as his face looks stressed and full of worry. He then says, "Anyway, enough about all that how was it with your colleagues, did they give you a hard time?"

Looking at his worried face I decide not to tell him. At least I can spare him one more worry this evening. Plastering a smile on my face I say, "Oh no everyone was fine. Luckily they know me and know that Nathan wasn't blameless in all of this. It will be fine so don't worry." He gives me a considered look and I squirm inside at his gaze. I don't think that I have fooled him but he doesn't press the matter. As I stand up to clear away he grabs hold of me. "Leave all that Bella. My housekeeper can deal with it in the morning. I have other plans for you." I swallow in anticipation. Even now with all this going on we have to be together. It's like our coping mechanism and I move towards him. He takes my hand and leads me upstairs.

As we get to the bedroom, he says, "Wait there Bella, I'm going to run you a nice relaxing bath first." He disappears off into the bathroom and I slowly undress and put on a robe. When he comes back I notice that he has stripped down to nothing. I can see that he is ready for me and his eyes darken as he sees me standing there. Gently he slips the robe from my shoulders and pulls me against him. He kisses me passionately and then leads me into the bathroom. We step into the bath and wash each other slowly. The steam from the bath and the sweet smelling oil that he has used adds to the intoxicating atmosphere. This is Ben at his most sensual. He is not going to rush anything and I know that we are in for a long night. I wasn't wrong. We spent the rest of the night just enjoying giving each other pleasure. We lit candles and massaged each other with oils. We took our time and just immersed ourselves in our need for each other. Lying in bed later on entwined together I feel so relaxed and content. This was just what the doctor ordered for both of us and nothing else matters. The world outside can't get in. We are safe.

I wake up and look at the clock by the bed. It is 3am and I notice that I am alone. Swinging my legs out of the bed I put on the discarded robe from earlier and go in search of Ben. Quietly I make my way downstairs and see a light on in his study. As I push open the door I can see him sitting in front of his laptop, a lamp giving off a low light nearby. As I enter the room he looks up and grins guiltily. "I'm sorry Bella, did I wake you? I tried to be quiet." Moving closer to him I reach over and touch his face gently. I push the screen of the laptop down and sit on his lap. Reaching up I kiss his lips gently and run my fingers through his hair. He groans and runs his hands underneath my robe and pulls me against him. I don't speak and let my body do the talking. Picking me up he pushes my robe to the ground. He kisses me all over and then lifts me up onto his desk, pushing the work onto the side and lays me back. I pull his clothes off and in no time at all he moves inside me. I arch towards him and I hear his breath coming in short sharp gasps. Then he explodes inside me and I feel him relax into me. Stroking his back I say, "Every time I catch you

working at 3am I will do my best to distract you. I want you with me at night Ben. Your work has you all day, at night you are mine." He pulls away and looks at me with passion in his eyes. "You are a welcome distraction Bella, but you are right, you must come first. Now let me return the favour." He pulls away and lifts me into his arms and with a wicked grin he hoists me over his shoulder and carries me off to bed.
When the alarm goes off at 6am we both groan. We have had two hours sleep. Ben was true to his word and I feel well and truly spent. The thought of another long day at work is not a welcome one. I jump in the shower and get ready. Then whilst he showers I race downstairs and grimace as I take in the mess that we left from last night. Trying not to let it bother me I set about making us some toast and cereal.

By the time Ben has come down I have made us breakfast and pour him a large mug of coffee. We don't have much time to linger and as we leave I say, "Look Ben, I'll drive myself today. You can get straight to work and then not have to worry about me. I'll pick us up something to eat later and we can just relax here tonight." I can tell that he is grateful and he kisses me gently on the lips. "I love you Bella, always remember that." "I love you too Ben and I will. Now go because I don't want you working when you get home and that's an order." He winks saying, "I'll deal with you later," and then races out of the door. Laughing to myself I follow him and head off to Kinghams with a heavy heart at the thought of the day ahead.

Chapter 3

Once again I have a bad day. To make matters worse April is away as she has to attend a funeral, so I don't even have my one remaining friend to talk to. Nobody is speaking to me and I isolate myself in my office and just do what I can. Luckily I have a few Reps to see which distracts me from my worries.

Although the system is up and running it is still not totally fixed and so everyone has to have their wits about them. The store has gradually been transformed since Ben took over and it is now much more modern and up to date. We are attracting a different sort of

customer and as I look around me I feel proud at what we have accomplished.

As I walk through the store to my department I see the department manager that Nathan was dating. I am not sure if they still are but I would have thought it unlikely after his appearance at the wedding.

As I walk past I expect her to throw me the usual evil glare that I am becoming accustomed to but instead she fixes me with a warm smile. Taken aback I return it with one of my own and am surprised as she heads towards me. She offers me her hand and says, "Its

Bella isn't it?" Smiling I shake her hand.
She carries on, "My name is Sophie. I don't think that we have been properly introduced." I must look

relieved and she says, "Look I don't want things to be awkward between us. I know that you have quite a history with Nathan but that is your business. I just wanted to let you know that I make up my own mind about people and as I don't know you personally I will withhold my judgement until I do." Smiling with relief I say, "Thank you Sophie. That means a lot to me. I am sure that whatever you have heard is not very good and I appreciate you telling me this. Things got a bit out of hand with Nathan but I wish him well and don't think badly of him."

Looking at me thoughtfully she says, "I know that he wishes more than anything that you hadn't broken up. I'm not stupid and despite the fact that we go on the odd date, I know that it is you he wants." I look at her in dismay.

"I'm sorry Sophie. I don't know what else I can do. You deserve better than that." She smiles and says brightly, "Yes I do, but nevertheless I enjoy his company so as long as I know the score I can deal with it." Anyway, I just wanted to say that I am glad to finally meet you and hope that we can get along." Looking at her standing there so open and honest I feel happy that Nathan has found somebody so sweet and kind. I am sure that he will forget about me the more time that he spends with her and I smile at her happily. "I would like that Sophie. Thank you, I'm glad that you said what you did." As we walk away from each other I feel surprised and just glad that she was so friendly. Maybe things would turn out for the better after all.

The day passes by with no more dramas and I pick up some food for dinner and head off home. I am starting to think of it as home now. I have taken on the cooking role as Ben is so busy and I just want to make sure that when he comes home he can relax and de-stress.

Happily I set about making us a nice meal and listen to music as I prepare everything. Ben called to say that he had been held up and would be back by 7.30pm so once the food is prepared and in the oven cooking I go up and have a relaxing bath and change into more comfy clothes. I think ahead to the weekend and feel happy as Phoebe and Boris are back from their honeymoon travels and I am moving my stuff out to give them space. I have got used to the idea now, probably due to the fact that I spend so much time here and it has started to feel more like home. It will be strange seeing all my things here and I am not looking forward to packing everything up but know it needs to be done.

When I get downstairs Ben is still not home so I decide to catch up on my emails. As soon as I log on I realise that something isn't right. The usual screen that greets me has changed and the words are jumbled up all over the place. I can't seem to get out of it and the screen freezes. Grabbing my I pad I try on there but it can't seem to connect to the site. In frustration I turn the laptop off and leave it. I'll take it in to Billy in the morning and he can deal with it. I hate IT problems. Hearing the front door open my heart skips a beat as Ben walks into the room. Despite the fact that he looks exhausted he is still gorgeous and I try to quell my lustful thoughts. As he grins at me I run over and jump in his arms. Laughing he hugs me to him and says, "That's a nice welcome." I kiss him and then pull away saying, "Go and get changed and I'll pour you a drink. Dinner's ready so hurry up." He laughs and says, "You are so demanding Bella, I may have to bring you into line later." I pretend to frown and say, "There will be none of that either tonight. You are going to chill out and relax and have an early night - to sleep. You need your sleep and we didn't get that

much last night if I remember." Winking sexily at me he says, "It will be fun disobeying you tonight Bella, you know that I can't resist you." I push him away and he goes off laughing to himself. Despite my good intentions I know that he is right. Who am I kidding that we will get an early night to sleep?

Chapter 4

As I make us breakfast the following morning I laugh to myself at the memory of the night before. I must have held out for about half an hour before he succeeded in his mission. I wonder if we will ever get tired of each other. I hope not, I have never ever been with anyone who turns me on as much as he does. Just one look is enough. I must try to find a way to channel my feelings otherwise I'll be worn out.

I remember to take my laptop and after saying goodbye to Ben I make my way to the store. I decide to drop the computer in to Billy first and then go to my office. It feels strange going in to what was once Nathan's office and I almost expect to see him in there. He hasn't been replaced yet and Billy is fielding most things and anything that he can't deal with gets referred to Head Office.

As I open the door Billy sees me and jumps out of his seat looking nervous. I smile at him reassuringly and say, "Hi Billy. Sorry to trouble you but can you look at my laptop for me? My emails have gone funny on it and I can't access them."

Billy looks worried and says, "It's not just you Bella. I have been taking calls ever since I arrived. Apparently it has affected everyone. I think we've been hit by a virus." I look at him in alarm. "Can you fix it?" I say hopefully. Shaking his head he says, "No, it's too big for me. I have referred it to Head Office so all of the computers are down today. The tills aren't affected as they run independently but I am afraid you will have to do without your computer until they can restore it all."

Nodding I say, "Ok, I'll wait until you say we can use them again." He answers another call and I head towards my office. I am really worried, not only did we have the problem with the tills but now we have a virus affecting the computers. I can't seem to shake off the feeling that Nathan is responsible and feel guilty as it is probably all down to me. I text Ben and tell him about the virus, although I am sure that he knows already. He texts me back and says that he knows and the whole group has been affected. He also says that he will be dealing with this all day and so may be late home again. Sighing to myself I realise that this is what my life will be like. He is so busy and has much to do all the time. No wonder he works into the night, he probably has to just to keep on top of everything. I am so cross with Nathan. I know that it is his fault and I just wish that I could lay into him.

It is surprising how reliant we are on computers and I spend much of the day sorting out paperwork in my office. April helps me out and soon it is lunch time. We decide to have ours together for a change in the staff canteen. I only go in there if April is with me as nobody will sit with me anymore. It's not just the stuff about Nathan. They think that I must tell Ben everything so don't want to compromise themselves. It is all getting really annoying now and once again I blame Nathan. We have a nice lunch and as we stand up to leave I notice Sophie at a table nearby. Telling April that I will catch her up I go up to Sophie's table. I can feel several pairs of eyes on me as everyone is probably curious as to what might happen. She smiles at me and I pull out a chair. "Hi Sophie, are you ok?" I start with. She nods and I carry on. "Listen, I'm sorry to ask but would you be able to pass on a message to Nathan for me?" Her eyes narrow and her smile slips slightly. "Yes if you like." she says, but I can tell that she feels awkward. "I'm sorry Sophie, I know it's probably difficult but I wonder if you could ask him to call me?" Seeing her expression I hastily say, "It's nothing about him and me, I can assure you. It's just computer related. I won't keep him long, but I'll

understand if he would rather not."
She smiles nervously and I say, "Thanks, I'm sorry to ask but it's kind of important." As I walk back to the office I feel bad. I don't want her to feel worried or awkward but I need to find out if Nathan is behind all of this. Within about ten minutes my phone rings. I don't recognise the number and answer it. Then I hear the familiar drawl and Nathan says softly, "Hi Bella. It's good to hear your voice." I am taken aback at how quickly he called me and it feels strange talking to him. I used to love hearing his voice but now I just feel detached from him. "So baby, what can I do for you," he says his tone gentle and caressing. Collecting myself together I say, "Nathan, please tell me that you haven't done anything to our computers." There is a pause and then he laughs softly. "Oh dear, are you

having problems then?"
Feeling exasperated I say shortly, "You already probably know that we are. If you have done anything then you had better put it right quickly. You will be the first person they call if the store reports it to the police." Nathan laughs louder this time and says, "As if I care about your problems at the store. I would like to see them try to link it to me. There is no evidence and they would only look bad in the eyes of their employees. It's not as if I haven't suffered enough is it?"
I feel very angry. I know it is him but he is obviously not going to do anything about it so I just cut off the call. There is no way I am going to give him any more satisfaction and regret calling him.
Feeling frustrated I return to my office and try to concentrate on work.

It must be about an hour later when the office door opens. April's expression changes to one of alarm and turning around I see Ben standing in the doorway. His

expression is grim and I suddenly feel uneasy.
Looking at April he smiles tensely. "Hi, its April isn't it?" she smiles and nods, words escaping her. He carries on, "I'm sorry but can I just have a private word with Bella?" She jumps up and says hurriedly, "I'll take my break now, no problem." Flashing me a nervous smile she scurries from the room.
As I look at him I suddenly feel nervous. His expression is grim and he stares at me as though

searching for something. Coming in he pulls April's seat over and sits down opposite me.

He gets straight to the point saying, "Bella, did you call Nathan today?" I swallow nervously and nod. He studies me and I feel as though I have done something

that I shouldn't. I am not sure why but I feel uncomfortable. Sighing he says, "Why do you look so worried Bella?"

I am taken aback and see that he looks concerned. "I don't know why." I reply, not quite meeting his eyes. Leaning forward he grabs hold of my hands. "Look at me Bella," he says softly. Looking up I see that his face has relaxed and he is smiling at me. "You never have to worry about telling me anything. I love you and you are the most important thing to me. In the back of your mind you probably remember the rumours about me and think that I am some kind of ogre, but I'm not Bella. The only people that should fear me are those who do something wrong or threaten

those I love. It is simple." My shoulders relax and I feel ashamed. He is right, there always seems to be a sense of fear that follows him. The reactions of other people have affected me and they shouldn't. I shouldn't fear him; after all he has never given me any reason to and has always been there when I needed him.

He can see that I have relaxed and gently says, "So tell me what you said to Nathan."

"I'm sorry Ben. I heard about the problems and

thought that it must have been him. I saw his girlfriend in the canteen and asked her to tell him to call me. He did so almost straight away and I asked him if he had caused our computer problems."

Ben looks thoughtful and says, "And did he?" Shrugging my shoulders I say, "Well obviously he denied it but I'm not so sure. I don't want to think that it's him but it all seems like too much of a coincidence." Ben nods saying, "Do you know how I know that you called him?" I am surprised because actually I hadn't thought about it, but now he comes to mention it I would like to know. Pulling out his phone he shows me a text. It is from Nathan and it was sent just after he phoned me. It just said that he shouldn't use his girlfriend to do his dirty work and next time be man enough to sort out his own problems. I can see him studying my reaction and I feel bad. "I'm sorry Ben," I say, meaning it. "I shouldn't have called him. I only wanted to help."

He shakes his head and his expression is grim. "The content of the text isn't the problem." I look at him in surprise and he says, "The problem is I never gave him my number. In fact this number is only used by a select few people. Most of my calls are directed to my secretary at Head Office."

"So what are you saying Ben?" I say wondering where this is going.

"I am worried that he has found a way of tapping into our phones or obtaining personal information. If that is the case then we are in a lot more trouble than I first realised."

I sit here stunned. Saying it like that sends shivers down my spine. He sees my expression and his face softens again. "Look don't worry about any of it. I will sort this out but I just want you to be vigilant. Don't tell anyone anything and be extra careful with your phone and computer. We can get past it; I just needed to find out what was said."

It then hits home how serious it must be for Ben to drop everything and come straight over. My eyes fill with tears and I feel bad. Ben pulls me up and holds me against him. "Come on Bella, it's not so bad. As long as we have each other nothing else matters." He kisses the top of my head and I sink into his embrace. As he holds me he says, "So this is your office hey. It's quite private really isn't it?" I push him away and laugh, "Don't even think about it," I say with mock anger. There is a hesitant knock on the door and I shout, "Come in." April peers around the door and her eyes widen as she sees that Ben is still here. He smiles and says, "Come in April, sorry to chase you out. I am afraid that I have come to ask Bella to leave with me. There's something we have to do." We both look at him in surprise and laughing he pulls me towards him saying. "I'm taking you shopping."

Chapter 5

As we walk through the store I am aware of several members of Staff watching us. I feel uneasy although I don't know why. It's not as though our relationship is

a secret anymore, but even so I feel awkward.
Ben doesn't hold my hand and we just walk together like any other co workers would do.
As soon as we get outside I let out a sigh of relief. Grabbing hold of my hand Ben grins at me saying, "Now you are mine." Laughing I feel relieved that all of the worry from before has left us and we stroll down the high street like any other couple would. As we walk I say, "Why are we going shopping Ben? It seems a bit strange when we're supposed to be

working." Grinning at me he says, "After the problems that we have had today and your subsequent telephone conversation I think that we need to re-

equip ourselves with new phones." Feeling surprised I ask, "Is it really that bad then?" He nods grimly. "For the time being we will both buy a pay as you go phone to use to call each other. It's just a precaution but a necessary one until we can get to the bottom of this. We will also set ourselves up with new email addresses and passwords just in case."
As I walk beside him I think about what he has just

said.

Soon we are at the phone store and he purchases two new phones and then pays with cash. We are issued with new numbers and once outside he says, "Ok, we will just use these to call each other. Still use your old one as normal and don't give anyone either of these numbers."

It all seems a bit extreme to me and I smile weakly at him, "Ok Ben, I understand."

He smiles and then lightens the mood by saying, "Come on, as I've got you to myself for once let's go for a coffee and try to put all of this behind us for an hour or so." Taking my hand we head for the nearest coffee shop. We chat about the coming weekend. I am moving my things in from Phoebe's flat and we work out how it's best to tackle it.

Then he holds my hand up to his lips and kisses it saying, "The weekend can't come soon enough for me Bella. The sooner you have moved in completely the better." Looking at him sitting there in front of me I feel very excited. Finally we can begin our lives together properly. Soon Ben looks at his watch and says, "Come on Bella, let's call it a day. I'll take you for dinner and then we can get home early for a change." I look at him in surprise and say, "But don't you have to work late because of the problems?" Laughing he says, "I have better qualified people than me to sort that mess out. Anyway, I just want to take my lady out for dinner. Work can take a back seat for once whilst I put you first for a change." Pulling me up he kisses me lightly on the lips and then whispers in my ear, "Even now I can't resist you. I'm almost tempted to skip the restaurant and just take you home to bed, but I must look after you, I don't want to make you ill." I look at him lovingly. I don't know why I felt so nervous earlier and I feel bad. He deserves more than that as he always looks after me so well.

The rest of the week passes by quickly and although they are not 100% fully fixed the computers are back up and running.

I am looking forward to the weekend; it will be nice to see Phoebe and Boris, although I do feel sad at the thought of moving out. We have lived together for three years and I have enjoyed every minute of it. Now she is married though I know that things must change.

On Saturday morning bright and early Ben and I drive to my old flat. We have arranged for a removal company to help move my larger items of furniture and the endless packing cases that I have filled with my clothes and bits and bobs.

As soon as we get there we notice that the Van is already there and making good progress, all supervised by Phoebe, holding aloft a clipboard as she organises it all. Seeing us coming she squeals and races towards us. "Bella, thank God, I've missed you so much." We squeeze the life out of each other and then she turns to Ben. I worry that things will be awkward but I needn't because as soon as she lets me go she launches herself at him and hugs him just as hard." He laughs and I can see that he is relieved. Linking her arms in ours she says, "Come in. Boris can make us all a drink and we can have a good old catch up. I've got loads of photos to show you of the wedding and honeymoon and you may be here for some time."

We get inside and Boris gives us a welcoming smile and kisses me and then shakes Ben's hand. "Come in you two, I've made the coffee and then when we've finished everything we can go to the pub for lunch." "But what about the removal company?" I say in alarm. "They will want us to get back so that they can unload." Phoebe waves her hands dismissively. "I've told them to store it for a few hours and to meet you back at yours at 4pm. Boris paid them overtime so they are more than happy." Boris winks at me and smiles saying, "Sorry guys, I have to do as my wife says don't I?" We all laugh and Ben says, "Well at least let me reimburse you Boris, you shouldn't be out of pocket on our behalf." Phoebe tuts and says, "Stop it Ben. Just let us do that for you as a leaving present." As she says the words we both look at each other and burst out crying. The two men laugh at us incredulously and through our tears Phoebe and I giggle at their expressions. We spend a lovely morning hearing all about their wedding and honeymoon. There are loads of photos and we look at every one, reminiscing about the day itself and commenting on the honeymoon ones. We head out to the pub for lunch and enjoy a nice lunch in the cosy pub. Despite Boris being initially unsure of Ben, I am pleased to see that he has obviously decided to give him a go which I am thankful for. I need my best friends to get on with my boyfriend and there appears to be no awkwardness at all. None of us mention Nathan and we have a lovely afternoon. The saddest part was saying goodbye to my old room and the flat. It all looks so empty and it is a wrench to leave the place that I have been so happy in. Ben leaves me to spend some time with Phoebe in my room and chats to Boris in the living room. Phoebe holds my hand and then hugs me, tears falling down her face. "Please keep your key Bella. You can come back whenever you want; in fact I insist that you come often." Hugging her back I say, "Thanks Phoebs. I love you and will always be close to you, even though we are not sharing anymore we will still call and see each other every week. Please promise me that?" Nodding frantically she says, "You better believe it." She stares at me for a second and then lowers her voice. "Listen Bella, I know that we haven't talked about what happened at the wedding with Nathan, but I just want you to know that I know it was a hard decision for you and I completely trust your judgement. Both Boris and I want you to be happy and will accept Ben completely. You know best and we trust your judgement. We will enjoy getting to know him and anything that has occurred before you met him can stay in the past. We will only judge him on his treatment of you." The tears fall freely down my face now and I hug her gratefully. "Thank you so much Phoebs. I do love him with all my heart and didn't even need to think about my decision. I am sure that you will grow to love him too."

There's a knock on the bedroom door and we spring apart wiping our eyes. Boris and Ben stand there laughing at us and Phoebe calls them over for a group hug. Then she says, "To the next chapter of our lives together."

Chapter 6

I soon settle in and due to the fact that Ben's house is so large my stuff doesn't take up much room at all. It feels good to have my things around me and I decide that when I next have time I must sort it all out properly.

Life is still hectic at the store and I have a feeling that we have not escaped from any more catastrophes.

It is a few weeks later when the real bombshell hits. Ben gets a call early in the morning and quickly jumps up getting ready in a hurry.

"What's wrong?" I say, worrying as I can see that Ben has turned pale. He continues getting ready quickly and says, "It appears that we may be the subject of breaking news. Apparently the details of every one of our customers and employees could have been obtained by hackers. I am not sure what the damage may be but it is all over the news. I need to get to the office to sort the mess out." My heart plummets and I feel worried. I don't want to hold him up and just as he leaves he says, "You may want to go to your parents or Phoebe's this evening as I am not sure if I'll be home and if I am it will be very late. Call me if you need to and I'll keep you informed." Then he stops and quickly rushes back. He pulls me tightly towards him and kisses me saying, "Don't worry Bella, I love you."

He races off before I can reply and my mind is reeling from what I have just heard.

Turning on the television I notice with a sinking feeling that it is just as he said. All over the news is the report that data may have been leaked from the Hardcastle group of stores and that people must be vigilant.

I know that this is bad. It will reflect badly on the store and will undoubtedly cost us customers. Once I get in to work I notice the gloomy faces of my fellow co workers. They look at me with unfriendly expressions which I am getting used to. Nobody talks to me anymore and I feel as if they all blame me for the problems that keep on hitting the store.

April is at her desk and she gives me a reassuring smile as I enter the room. "More bad news Bella," she says looking at me with a sympathetic smile. Nodding I say, "It appears so. Maybe we should set about changing our passwords and login details for our private accounts?" Shaking her head she says, "I already have. You can't be too careful these days, what with all the cyber crime out there." Despite feeling so despondent I laugh to myself. April is always such a pessimist. She thinks that everything will happen to her and always looks on the worst side.

We try to continue with business as usual.

After work I decide to go and see my parents. I haven't seen them for a while and could do with catching up with them. Ben texted me earlier to say that he would be really late and I don't feel like going home to the large empty house on my own, just to watch the bad news on the television.

Once I get to my parents house I am pleased to see that at least some people are glad to see me. I join them for dinner and they talk about the news and then the conversation turns to Phoebe's wedding. I know that they wanted me to choose Nathan and that they were disappointed that I went with Ben. They have never said as much and are always welcoming to him, but I know that they don't respond to him the same way as they did Nathan. I tell myself that they will grow to love him as much as I do once they get to know him, but I just wish it wasn't so awkward.

As we watch the television the phone rings and I hear my mother talking to somebody, and by the sounds of it the conversation is quite fraught. As she comes back into the room I can see that she looks worried and her face is full of concern.

"What is it Janet?" my father says as she sinks down on to the settee.

"It's Nathan," she says looking at me in alarm. I feel a terrible sense of foreboding and say, "What is it, is he ok?" Shaking her head she says, "That was Maria, apparently he has been arrested." I look at her in disbelief as she carries on.

"He was taken in for questioning in relation to the problems at Hardcastles. It appears that everyone connected to the IT departments of the stores, past and present are being questioned." I feel a sense of relief at her words. It sounds as though it is just standard procedure. Despite my own thoughts I know that he wouldn't be involved in anything this big. This has gone way past just getting even with Ben, this is

criminal. Smiling reassuringly at her I say, "I'm sure that he will be fine. It sounds as if they are questioning everyone as routine procedure. They will soon see that it wasn't him." My mother looks worried still and says, "I hope so for his sake. Maria is extremely worried and doesn't know how much more he can take."

I look down feeling as if they all blame me. My parents don't say it but I know that they blame me for Nathan's problems. The fact that he lost me and his job and that now he has been arrested won't make them warm to Ben anytime soon. I don't say anything else and keep quiet. This is all a complete nightmare and I wish that things would return to normal for all our sakes.

Later on that evening I return home and the house is in darkness. It is 9pm so I have a nice bath and try to relax. Soon I hear the crunch of gravel on the drive and realise that Ben is home. Quickly I jump out of the bath and grabbing a robe race downstairs to greet him. He looks at me approaching and I notice his strained and tired expression. Flinging myself at him I crush him to me. His arms pull me tightly against him and we stand there for a few minutes just glad to be together. Pulling back I say, "Come on, let me get you something to eat and drink. You can jump in my bath if you like and try to relax." He smiles and says, "I love coming home to you Bella. It makes sense of my life. Without you I have nothing." Tears come into my eyes and I kiss him gently. I softly say, "Go on, take your time. You don't have to talk about work if you don't want to." I watch as he heads off upstairs and then set about making him some pasta. As I watch him eat I notice that he appears a little more relaxed than when he first came in.

I sit with him and whilst he eats tell him about Nathan. He looks at me for a while and then says, "I know." Looking at him in surprise I wait for him to explain and he sighs and pushes his plate away. "Look Bella, everybody who has been involved with our computer systems have been questioned. Nathan's name came up several times and the email that he sent to all of the staff was mentioned. They believe that he is a suspect and had a motive. It's in their hands now and if he is innocent then he will be released. If they find out that he was responsible then he will be charged and would probably go to prison." He looks at me for my reaction and my face must show my dismay. Reaching over he grabs my hands and says, "If it's worth anything, I think that he will be released." Pulling me up he holds me against him. "I know that you don't wish him ill Bella that is what I love about you. You are kind hearted and I don't ever want you to change. It's natural to feel worried about him; after all you were very close for a while. Those feelings don't just disappear overnight and I am not expecting them to." I pull back and smile, reaching up to touch his face. "I wish everyone knew you as I do Ben. You're kind of special yourself." I kiss him gently at first and then with more passion. He is right, I am concerned for Nathan. If he is innocent then all will be well, and if he isn't then he must suffer the consequences.

Chapter 7

My mother calls me the next day to say that Nathan was released without charge. I feel relieved that it wasn't him and breathe a huge sigh of relief. The investigation is still open and I just hope that they find who was responsible. The fallout is still happening though and Ben is once again locked into meetings until late.

The next few days are the same and I am beginning to wonder if life will ever return to normal. Ben is still stressed and I am still finding it difficult at work. We don't spend much time together and because I am living with him I don't even have anyone to talk to when I go home. We can't arrange to go anywhere for a break because it is all still up in the air at work.

About a week later I go to grab a sandwich from the deli on the corner for lunch. I am avoiding the staff canteen now, not just due to the dirty looks but also to get out of the store for an hour to clear my head.

As I am lining up to pay I feel a tug on my arm. Swinging around I am startled to see Nathan standing there. A broad smile breaks out onto his face and he says, "Bella, I thought I saw you coming in here. It's good to see you baby."

I continue to stare at him in amazement. It's like he only saw me yesterday and that nothing has happened. Recovering I smile and say, "Nathan. What a surprise. What brings you here. I thought that you had taken another job with Bradley?" Before he can answer I have to pay. Once I have he grabs my arm and says, "Wait for me Bella. It would be good to catch up." Even though I don't want to I realise that it would be rude not to so wait nervously for him.

He propels me over to a table and we sit there facing each other awkwardly. Looking at me with a gentle expression he says, "It's good to see you Baby. I've missed you." Blushing I look down. I can't believe that he is talking to me like this and I say, "Nathan, it's good to see you. I am sorry to hear that you were arrested over the computer problems. When I heard that you had been cleared of it I was glad." A flicker of irritation crosses his face and he says, "Yes, it wasn't a pleasant experience but I expected it." Nodding I don't know what else to say about it so I move on to safer ground.

"How are your parents? I feel bad that I haven't spoken to them since we split up, but I do miss them and I know that your mum still talks to mine."

He studies me intently and replies, "They love you like a daughter. They still do, it appears that none of us can switch off our feelings off for you." I blush feeling nervous and wish that I hadn't seen him.

All of a sudden he puts his hand over mine and I look up at him in surprise. His eyes are burning as they look at me and he says, "I know that you have moved on Bella but I can't. I know that I am seeing Sophie, but she is not you and it is very casual. I was a fool and have regretted it every day since. I came here on purpose today in the hope that I would see you. When I saw you leave I followed you here because I wanted to tell you in person that I will wait for you. I am sure that you will soon find out that Ben is not the man for you. We were meant to be together and I am not giving up on us. When you are ready I will be

waiting." Pulling my hand away I quickly stand up. "Please Nathan, you must move on. This isn't healthy for either of us. Sophie seems a lovely girl; you should give her more of a chance. Ben and I are fine and I am not going to leave him. Please don't contact me again." Softening my voice I say, "It's for the best, you will see that sooner rather than later, I hope so for your sake."

Quickly I push my way out of the deli and hurry outside. But Nathan doesn't give up and rushes after me. Catching me up he pulls me against him crushing me against him. I feel his familiar embrace and can hear his heart beating. I try to get away but he is too strong. Before I can stop him he grabs hold of my hair and pulls my face against his, kissing me in a deep and passionate way. I can't move away because he is too strong and tears run down my face at how helpless I am. I don't know what to do and the only thing I can think of is to stamp on his foot with as much force as I can muster. It takes him by surprise and he relaxes his hold. Pulling away I slap him forcefully around the face and then without saying anything at all run as fast as I can back to the store.

As soon as I reach the sanctuary of my office I close the door and lean back against it. Tears are running down my face and I can't seem to stop them. I feel as if I am in a nightmare that I can't wake up from. Why won't he leave me alone?

Once again I go home to an empty house. I start preparing the dinner and Ben texts to say he will be back by 8pm. As I look around me I feel so alone. I could go to my parents but I feel awkward talking to them as it is obvious that they don't like Ben much. Phoebe is away again visiting friends and I realise that most of my other friends were also Nathan's, so I have sort of lost touch with them all.

I start to watch a film as I wait for him but I can't concentrate. The house feels so big and empty. We are in the middle of nowhere and I will have to drive if I want to go anywhere. I am finding it hard to see a way out of this and decide that I will try to get Ben to take a couple of days off to go away somewhere. I think that it would do us both the power of good.

He gets home just after 8pm and we follow the same pattern. We have our meal and talk about work. I pretend that all is well so that I don't add to his worries. I decided against telling him about Nathan's visit; it would only wind him up anyway and I just want a stress free evening. Whilst we sit in front of the television I broach the subject of a few days away. He has his arm around me and I am enjoying the feeling

of him so close to me which is comforting. He thinks about what I said for a minute and then says, "I would love to Bella, you know that. Once this is all over we will make plans to go away for the weekend. You choose, anywhere at all." Sighing I say, "The trouble is that even if this does go away, something else is bound to replace it. I don't spend as much time as I would like with you and just thought that a weekend away would do us both good." Pulling me on to his lap he holds me gently, stroking my hair. "I'm sorry Bella. I know that I have neglected you and I'm sorry. Let me make it up to you. I will organise a weekend away for us in two weeks time. It will be a surprise and I promise that you will have the time of your life. But for now, let me reassure you that you are my first priority." He bends towards me and kisses me deeply and passionately. I know where this is all going as it's his answer to everything. Suddenly I feel annoyed. I pull away and get off his lap. He looks surprised and I say harshly, "I'm sorry Ben but I want more than that. You know that I want you and it's your answer to everything. The trouble is I need for us to have more than just sex. We come home, have dinner and then go to bed. We need to have a life together outside of the bedroom too." I don't know why but I suddenly burst out crying and rush upstairs. I lock myself in the bathroom and let it all out. I know that I am not just crying because of tonight, it is more than that. It's as

though everything has built up to this point. The break up with Nathan, moving out of the flat into here, the problems at work and the hostility. I think about the meeting with Nathan and how helpless I felt. Then I think about my life now, I am lonely and despite loving Ben more than I ever thought possible I am

realising that it just isn't enough.
I don't hear him come upstairs but all at once I hear him outside the door. "Please unlock the door Bella. Let me in." I sit there wanting to let him in but also needing to get this out of my system. I don't answer and he repeats it again. "Let me in, we need to sort this out."
Wiping my eyes and blowing my nose I unlock the door. He comes into the bathroom and taking my hand he pulls me down against him, sitting on the floor, his back to the bath. Stroking my hair he puts his arms securely around me. I feel like a child as he rocks me gently, giving me little feather light kisses on my head. He says softly, "Its ok Bella, let it all out. Cry for as long as you need to. I'm here and I am not going to leave you until you have let it all out." It's like I am a child again and gradually my sobbing subsides and I calm down. We must sit on the floor of the bathroom for an hour. We don't talk just sit there together in silence. I feel safe and secure and then a little foolish. I can't believe that I let myself go like that. I'm not even sure where it came from. One thing I do know for sure is that I am going to get a grip. A hysterical girlfriend is not what Ben needs at the moment and despite all of this I am going to have to come up with another reason as to what's the matter. I must be strong for him as this must be just as difficult for him, if not more so given his responsibility. Starting to feel ashamed I say in a small voice, "I'm sorry Ben. I didn't mean to lose control like that. I must just be tired and stressed and it all got to me." He pulls me

away from him and looks into my eyes.

I will myself not to crumble and after a moment he says, "Come on, lets go downstairs and I will make you a cup of tea. Let's just sit and talk this evening and not talk about work. We will make plans to do something together this weekend. It's about time that you came first, I can see that this has all affected you and you need a break."

The rest of the evening passes by calmly. We decide to book a mini break to the Lake District and then have an early night and just cuddle together in bed.

Chapter 8

The week soon passes and Ben picks me up from work on the Friday. We are going to drive up to the Lake District, where we have booked a hotel break for two nights. We packed last night and our bags are already in the boot.

I feel excited and am very much looking forward to a change of scene. However to my surprise Ben drives towards my old flat instead of the motorway. I look at him in surprise and say, "Why are we here?" Winking he says, "I thought that you may like some company. I realised the other night that I have been selfish in keeping you to myself, locked up in an ivory tower. I invited Phoebe and Boris to come with us."

I can't believe it and a broad grin breaks out onto my face. Flinging my arms around him I kiss him repeatedly. "Thank you, thank you. I can't believe it." I laugh as I see Phoebe running at full pelt towards the car and Boris struggling behind her with their bags. Jumping out I hug my friend and Ben goes to help Boris. Phoebe cries, "Surprise! We are hijacking your romantic weekend away." Laughing I say, "I'm so happy that you have. This is the best surprise that I could wish for." Phoebe and I jump in the back so that we can chatter all the way there. I can see Ben throwing us amused looks as he drives and I feel so full of love for him. I feel bad that I caused such a scene and vow to myself that I will never do it again. Phoebe and I chat all the way and soon we are turning into the drive of a magnificent country hotel. It looks amazing and I feel so excited. We park the car and take our bags to the reception. Ben has booked us amazing rooms and as we unpack I look in amazement at the beautiful surroundings. "Ben, this room is gorgeous. It must have cost a fortune," I say running over and planting a big kiss on his cheek. He raises his eyes up and says, "You will have to do better than that Bella." Laughing I kiss him again, this time on the lips with as much restraint as I can manage. He pulls me in and kisses me harder and then sweeps me off my feet and throws me unceremoniously on to the four poster bed. He pins me beneath him and says seductively, "I can think of lots of uses for a four poster bed." Raising my eyes I say, "I shall look forward to you showing me then." He rolls off and laughs and I am glad to see that he is more relaxed than he has been and a shiver of excitement runs through me at the thought of what he has in store later. We quickly change and meet Phoebe and Boris downstairs for dinner. They are as bowled over as we are over the hotel and we have a delicious dinner in the restaurant and drink far too much wine. I love spending time with them as they make me laugh and I am very grateful to Ben for inviting them. It was just what I needed and once again I am amazed at how well he reads me.

After dinner we sit in the lounge and have coffee and brandies. There is a roaring fire and it feels so cosy. In no time at all we all start yawning and decide to head off to bed. I run a bath as soon as we get in the room and add some relaxing oil that is provided. As soon as it is ready I call Ben in and say, "Bath's ready." He comes into the bathroom and I am lying in the bath. Smiling seductively at him I start lathering the soap all over me holding his gaze the whole time. I see his eyes darken and can tell that I have his full attention. He just stands there and watches as I carry on. Then when he can bear it no more he removes his clothing and joins me in the bath, pulling me to him and kissing me passionately. He shifts my body so that I am sitting between his legs and taking the soap from

my hands he gently moves it all over my body. Taking it back from him I do the same to him. Wrapping my legs around him I pull in closer to him. He pushes forward until I am lying back in the bath and he moves inside me, holding me to him with one hand and holding on to the edge of the bath with the other. He gently thrusts inside me until I can bear it no more. Then just as I am on the edge he pulls out and pulls me up. My body feels on fire and he pulls me out of the bath and wraps a towel around me. My body is screaming out in frustration and he smiles wickedly at me. Sweeping me up he takes me to the bed and lays me down. Still holding my gaze he once again grins wickedly at me and then produces two ties from the side of the bed. My eyes widen as he gently ties both of my wrists to the posts on the bed. He laughs at my expression and then proceeds to torture me by kissing and touching my body, knowing that I cannot move or touch him in return. I start to plead with him, "Please Ben, I can't take any more. I need you." Grabbing hold of my hair he pulls my head towards him and kisses me gently at first and then with more passion. Then just in time he enters my body and I feel the waves of release crashing over me as we climax together.

Rolling over he laughs at me still tethered to the bed. "I think I may leave you there for my own enjoyment," he teases and I feel shy and embarrassed. Seeing my obvious discomfort he releases me laughing and pulls me over until I am on top of him. He strokes my hair back from my face and says, "I love you Bella. You know that I would never do anything to hurt you don't you?" Nodding I kiss him again. I love him so much. I don't think that I will ever tire of him. We lay wrapped up in each other and soon drift off to sleep.

Chapter 9

The next morning we meet up with Phoebe and Boris for breakfast at 9am. Deciding to go for a long walk we meet up outside once we have changed into our walking gear. As we set off I am just grateful that it is a lovely day. Walking along we chat about anything and everything and have well and truly caught up by the time we come across a little tea rooms next to the lake.

Heading off inside we order full cream teas all round and eat far too much and are just glad that we can walk it all off on the way back. I am pleased to see that Ben and Boris appear to be getting along. Boris is far more relaxed with him and I even hear them swapping stories on funny things that happen in the banking world.

On the way back to the hotel I link arms with Phoebe and we lag a bit behind the men.

"I am glad to see that Ben and Boris are getting on." I say happily. Smiling she says, "Yes, Boris told me that he was going to give him the benefit of the doubt. All of those stories are as Ben said just rumours. He said that he would prefer to make up his own mind about him instead."

"I'm glad; I knew that you would both like him if you just got to know him." Grinning at me she says, "Well he is gorgeous, so he can't be all bad." Giggling like schoolgirls we laugh even more as they turn around and throw us amused looks.

When we get back to the hotel Ben surprises Phoebe and me by saying, "I have booked you both into the spa for the afternoon. You have a massage followed by a facial and manicure and pedicure. That should keep you both out of mischief whilst Boris and I have a round of golf." Looking at him in surprise I say, "I never knew you played golf Ben, do you even have any clubs?" Laughing he says, "Yet another talent of mine Bella and yes I do have some clubs but not here. We have both hired a set and are looking forward to a nice relaxing game." Boris and Phoebe laugh at my expression and I realise that they were also in on this. Jumping up I hug him tightly. "Thank you Ben. This break just gets better and better."

"Anything for you Bella," he whispers and then kisses me softly.

We all go to our rooms and change ready for our activities. As I sit on the bed watching Ben get ready I say, "I love you Ben. You have given me such a lovely surprise and I feel bad for falling apart on you the other night." He races over and sits in front of me, kneeling on the floor. Taking my hands in his he says, "No I am sorry Bella. I should have realised the pressure that you were under. You have been through a lot lately and I didn't understand how difficult it all was for you to adjust to. This is just my way of making it up to you and saying that I will put your needs before anything else. Just remember to trust me." Tears come into my eyes and he pulls me against him. He strokes my hair and I feel so loved.

Pulling away he says with a grin, "Anyway, the others will be waiting and you have an afternoon of pampering to look forward to."

Phoebe and I sit together waiting for our pamper session to begin. We are wearing white towelling robes and have been given Champagne to drink. Stretching out on the beds that are side by side I say, "I could so get used to living like this." Phoebe laughs and says, "So could I. Wasn't Ben clever to think of this?" I smile happily and say, "Its strange how things have changed for us both isn't it? I mean you and Boris are married and living at our flat that we shared and I am with Ben now and living in the middle of nowhere." Phoebe agrees and then says, "Actually, things have changed even more for me just lately." I look at her in surprise and she blushes and says, "Boris and I are moving. We have bought a house in a village not far from you." Looking at her in amazement I say, "I can't believe it. Tell me everything." She blushes again and says, "We decided that as much as we love living at the flat we would really like to start our married life living more in the country. We would like to get a dog or two and move away from the town. We are going to keep the flat and rent it out. I couldn't bear to sell it; we have such

happy memories there after all." Smiling I say, "I'm glad that you are keeping it. You're right we did have such fun there. It's great that you will be nearer though. I find it quite lonely out in the middle of nowhere, and if you aren't far away then I can come around to yours when Ben is working." She looks at me and I notice her expression change. "Tell me Bella, is it working out for you living there?"

Looking down I say, "I do feel a bit isolated sometimes. I had a bit of a meltdown in the week which is why Ben organised this break. I feel bad but everything got on top of me and I broke down."

Phoebe looks dismayed and reaches out to grab my hand. "You should have told me Bella. You know that I would happily come and keep you company or you could come to ours. You could stay in your old room. You never have to feel alone." I nod my head and feel ashamed again.

The trouble with Phoebe is that she knows me so well and says, "So tell me what's really bothering you?" Sighing I tell her about my meeting with Nathan and the awful atmosphere at work. Her eyes widen and she says, "You have to tell Ben. He needs to know. You can't bottle it all in." Vehemently I shake my head and say, "No, he has so much to deal with at the moment. I can cope as long as I have him and you two to talk to. I just needed to let off steam, but I am fine now." We are interrupted by two ladies who come to give us our treatments and the conversation stops for a while whilst we just enjoy the experience.

Once Phoebe and I have been well and truly pampered we go to look for the guys. Typically we find them in the bar and we join them for a drink. Ben puts his arm around my shoulders and says, "How was it Bella, do you feel relaxed now?" Smiling up at him I say, "Well

and truly. Thank you Ben it was a lovely surprise.
"Phoebe adds, "Yes, just what the doctor ordered. The trouble is Boris, I could get used to this sort of treatment so be warned." We all laugh and Boris raises his eyes up and then plants a loving kiss on her excited face. "Anything for you P," he says, gazing at her adoringly. Ben grins at me and we laugh. I say, "Oh no, you've started something now Ben, Boris is certainly going to feel the pressure now."
We all head off to our rooms to get changed for dinner. As we get ready I say, "How was golf with Boris, did it all go ok?" He nods and says, "Yes, Boris is good company and I think that all the awkwardness has gone, at least I hope so." Smiling I say, "I am glad. He is lovely and it would have been difficult if there was an atmosphere between you."
I feel so happy. This is more like it. Life feels normal again and I am so glad that Ben invited them to come with us. I feel as though I can cope with the stresses back at work now that we have had this break.
As it's our last night we push the boat out and order Champagne with our meal. We have a really good time and Phoebe and Boris tell us all about their new house. We promise to help them move in and I feel happy that they will be living closer to us. The evening draws to a close and we all turn in, exhausted from our busy day.

I am woken by the sound of Ben's phone ringing. It is

early in the morning and I wonder who could be ringing him so early. I see him frown as he looks at the display and jumps out of bed to answer it. His tone is short and he just says, "Yes." I can hear somebody speaking but can't make out what they are saying. All he says is, "Ok," and then hangs up. His face is blank and gives nothing away. "Who was that?" I say sitting up and watching him. He puts the phone back down and his face relaxes again as he jumps back into bed. "Nobody important, just work stuff." He pulls me close and says, "Oh well, now we're awake we mustn't waste any more of our precious time together."

By the time we meet the others for breakfast I think that Ben must have exhausted all of his uses for a four poster bed. I actually feel like I need to go back to sleep for another 24 hours after this morning, however I am now famished and can't wait for a big breakfast. Phoebe notes my flushed face and grins knowingly at me which makes me blush even more.

We have to check out by 10am so reluctantly pack our bags and decide to have a slow drive home. Once again Phoebe and I sit in the back and chat about general things until Ben pulls into a service station for us to stretch our legs and get a coffee. Phoebe and I go to the ladies and as we wash our hands she says, "Look Bella, it's difficult to talk properly with the boys listening. Why don't we meet up this week for a drink after work? I feel as though we need to talk more about what is going on with you at the moment."

I look at her gratefully and say, "Oh Phoebs, I would love to. I miss having you to sound off to. Why don't we grab a pizza on Tuesday?" "Great, I'll meet you at the usual Pizza restaurant at 6pm then." I feel so happy that we have something in the diary and we go back out to join the others. Ben notices that I have brightened up and smiles at me as he sees us coming. He squeezes my hand when we reach them and whispers, "I'm pleased to see that you look much happier now." I look up at him and think how lucky I am to have him.

Chapter 10

With a heavy heart I return to work on Monday. The weekend was fabulous but now I have to concentrate on the job in hand. At least I have my dinner date with Phoebe to look forward to.

April is in good spirits and regales me with tales of her weekend spent decorating. "I'm glad to come back to work for a rest," she exclaims, picking paint off of her hand. Looking hard at me she says, "You look better than you did last week Bella. Did you do anything nice?" I nod and tell her all about my weekend. By the time I finish she looks well and truly jealous. "God you're so lucky. The best Tom can manage is a night in his parent's caravan in Dorset." We burst out laughing and then look at what we have to do for the rest of the day. I notice that I have some letters to open and soon come across a white envelope that looks unlike the usual correspondence that I get at work. As I open it I pull out a single sheet of A4 paper with just a couple of lines typed onto it. My blood runs cold as I read what it says - BELLA, DO YOU KNOW WHAT YOUR BOYFRIEND REALLY DOES AFTER WORK?

I look over at April but she hasn't seen me open it and is engrossed in her computer screen. My heart starts beating fast and my mind starts racing as I try to think who the sender could be. I can't concentrate and just

sit there thinking about the letter. After a while I fold it up and put it in my bag. I'll put it out of my mind and show it to Phoebe tomorrow night. I decide not to say anything to Ben. I don't want to spoil our first night back after the lovely time we have just had.
I throw myself into work and put it to the back of my mind. The day goes by quite quickly and when I get home I am amazed to see that Ben is already there. As soon as I get through the door he comes to meet me and swings me around. I laugh as he says, "Surprise. I thought that it was my turn to cook for you for a change and made sure that I beat you to it." "This is a pleasant surprise," I say happily. He grins and says, "Go and get changed whilst I dish up. I have made your favourite, Coq au Vin." Racing off to change I am glad that he appears to be still in a relaxed and happy mood.

We have a lovely dinner and he doesn't mention work once. We chat about the weekend and about Phoebe and Boris's impending move. Once we have finished he says, "Come on, I'm taking you out for a drink." I look at him in surprise. "This is unexpected." He winks and says, "I need to take you out more. The trouble is I can't keep my hands off you when we're here so if we go out you stand more of a chance." I giggle and nod my head in agreement. "Come on then, where are you taking me?" "Oh just to the local pub. I may only be able to manage one drink before the temptation gets too much and I whisk you back here."

I raise my eyes up and we head off to the local.

The pub is busy but we manage to find a table and squash together on the bench. The atmosphere is cosy and I am interested to see the different people that make up the local community. Because we are working all the time we haven't even met our nearest neighbours. There are all sorts of people here and a multitude of different breeds of dogs. I like the pub and would enjoy getting more involved in community life given half a chance. After an hour, true to his word Ben whispers, "Sorry Bella, I can't stand it anymore. I need to get you home. Maybe we can manage longer tomorrow?"

Laughing say, "I won't be here tomorrow remember. I am meeting Phoebe after work for a pizza." He pulls a face and says, "Then we have no time to waste." Giggling like teenagers we race off home.

Ben has to go in early in the morning so is gone before I get up. I laugh thinking back to last night. Once again we didn't get much sleep and I think with amusement of how tired he must be feeling now. Once I get into work I notice another letter like the one from yesterday, waiting for me and I open it with trepidation. As before there are just a few words typed onto the paper that read:

BELLA, HE IS NOT THE PERFECT BOYFRIEND THAT YOU THINK HE IS.

My heart starts racing again and I feel sick. The words don't worry me but the thought that someone out there is taking the time to send me these vile letters does.

They are probably hoping to break Ben and I up. The anger grows within me and I think of Nathan. It must be him, who else could it be? He is the only one who would benefit from us splitting up. I decide to do nothing. That is what he wants so I will not give him the satisfaction. If I ignore them then no damage can be done. I know in my heart that none of it is true. Well if they want to waste their time then let them.

Chapter 11

As I enter the restaurant I can see that Phoebe is already waiting for me at a table in the corner. She looks up and smiles as I approach. On seeing my expression her smile is replaced by an anxious look. Jumping up she says, "What's the matter Bella? Sit down and tell me everything." I should have known that she would sense that something was wrong but this was even quicker than I had anticipated. Before I can even sit down though the waiter approaches so we set about ordering some drinks first.

Once the waiter leaves she looks at me questioningly. Sighing I pull the letters from my bag and hand them over to her saying, "These were sent to me, one yesterday and one today." As she reads them her expression turns to horror. "This is sick," she exclaims, "Have you shown them to Ben yet?" I shake my head and she looks at me with exasperation. "I thought that you were going to tell him everything from now on. Why haven't you. He needs to know?" "Because he was in such a good mood yesterday. I didn't want to upset him again. Also this one only came today." Phoebe looks at me and says seriously, "Do you think it's Nathan?" I nod saying, "Who else could it be? But I don't want to dredge it all up again. If I ignore them then he hasn't won and will stop."

The waiter arrives with the drinks and I see Phoebe deep in thought. We order our pizzas and when we are alone again she says, "Well you must show him tonight. Even if nothing is done about it at least you both know the situation." She is right of course. I don't even know why I didn't mention it yesterday. Putting the letters away I force a smile on my face and say, "Anyway, let's not talk about it anymore. I want to hear all about your new house." Phoebe tells me everything and it all sounds great. "You must take me to see it Phoebs. After all you need my seal of approval as well."

"Of course, when are you next off, we could go then." We decide to go on Sunday and then I say, "I know. You and Boris could come to us for Sunday lunch. It would be great and give me something to look forward to." Phoebe smiles with excitement and then says, "But will Ben mind? Do you want to check with him first?" I shake my head, "No, we don't have any plans so I'm sure he will be fine about it. If there is a problem I'll let you know." That settled we chat about general things and have a lovely evening.

I get home and resolve to tell Ben about the letters. However when I get in I have to go looking for him and find him working away hard in the study. As he looks up I can see how tired and worried he looks. Grinning ruefully he says, "Sorry Bella. I'm glad that you went out tonight because it looks as if this is going to take some time." I smile at him and push all thoughts of the letters to the back of my mind. Now is obviously not the time and he looks distracted anyway.

"Ok Ben, I'll give you a pass for tonight. Let me make you a drink and then I'm going to have a bath." I go over and kiss him lightly and then leave him to it.
It doesn't take long to make the drinks and once I have given him his I take mine up to the bathroom. I let the water work its magic and feel more relaxed after my bath.
I get ready for bed and head off downstairs to say goodnight to Ben. As I approach the study I can hear him talking to somebody in hushed tones. He sounds angry though and something tells me that this would not be a good time to go in. I can't really hear much but his voice rises slightly and I hear him say, "I know what you want but it's not going to happen. She stays with me, end of."
I know I shouldn't eavesdrop but I can't help myself. Inching closer I listen carefully, straining to hear. I then hear, "What about Scorpio, hasn't she found them yet?" The other person is obviously speaking and then he says, "Well you're not using Bella. I don't care what you want, she must never find out any of it." I back away in confusion. Quietly I tiptoe back upstairs and once I reach the sanctuary of our room I sit on the bed trying to process what I just heard. Soon I hear footsteps and grabbing a brush I start to brush my hair. Ben comes into the room and I can see that his expression is strained. Mustering a smile I say, "You look like you need an early night, can't you leave the

work until the morning?" Coming over he sits beside me. He pulls me towards him and holds me tightly against him. I can feel him burying his face in my hair and can feel the tension in him. Pulling away I stroke the side of his face and say, "What's wrong Ben? Please tell me. You look as if you need to tell someone. Is it the stores?"

He appears to shake himself and then his face is set in a more controlled expression. "I'm sorry Bella. It's been a hell of a day and no the work can't wait until tomorrow. I just wanted to escape from it for five minutes to hold you." He looks gently into my eyes and says, "Just know that I love you Bella, I always have and always will. I will do anything for you, please remember that."

A lump forms in my throat and I think back to the conversation that I overheard. There is something that concerns me that he isn't telling me. For whatever reason he is trying to protect me, that much is evident. I pull him to me. I must be as strong for him. I will do anything to protect him too. Kissing him gently I say, "I know you do Ben and I love you too, always remember that." We just sit there hugging for a while and then he reluctantly pulls away and heads back downstairs to his study.

Chapter 12

I am not even sure if Ben comes to bed at all and when I wake up he is gone. He has left me a note saying that he had to go in early and would probably be late home and would call me later on.

With a heavy heart as I get ready I can't get the conversation that I overheard out of my mind. I know that something is going on but am baffled as to what it can be.

I head off to work and arrive to find April already there. She offers a cheery hello and then says, "Sorry Bella, I have to go to IT for training today on the new system. Will you be alright without me?" Smiling I say, "Yes of course, don't worry. I hope it's not too boring." Laughing she raises her eyes and disappears off.

With a heavy heart I see another envelope like the other two. This one looks as though it was hand delivered as there is no stamp. With trepidation I open it. As I unfold the letter I notice a photograph has been printed on to it. My heart nosedives as I see that it was taken at our house. The front door is open and Ben is standing there with a woman. It looks like it was taken last night because I can see that he is wearing the same clothes that he had on when I came home. She has her hand on his face stroking the side of it. I cannot see her face but she has short dark hair and is wearing a camel coloured coat. Ben looks strained but has a weak smile on his face as he looks at her. The note says,

WHILST THE CAT'S AWAY!

I feel sick. They are obviously insinuating that something is going on between them. I wonder why Ben never mentioned it. He was certainly in a mood last night and I just put it down to the work, but suddenly things don't seem so cut and dried anymore. Then a terrible thought strikes me, whoever is sending these letters knows where we live. A feeling of dread comes over me and my mind starts whirring.

The phone that Ben bought for me suddenly beeps and I see a text from him. It says- Bella. Come to head office right away. I need to see you urgently.

Feeling extremely worried and apprehensive I leave the store. I don't tell anyone and am grateful that April is on the course. Luckily I have no appointments scheduled for the day so don't have to ring anyone to cancel.

On the way over I run through everything in my mind. I feel worried about what I will find. I have never been summoned to his office before. I haven't even been to head office, which is strange really considering that he works there. As I wander through the store I realise how different it is to Kinghams. The general feeling is one of top quality and everything is pristine and modern. The staff look well polished and professional. I make my way to the customer services desk and see a smart looking receptionist manning the desk. As I approach she smiles at me and I say, "I have come to see Ben Hardcastle." She looks at me with a slight frown and says, "Is he expecting you?" I nod nervously and she says, "Please tell me your name and I will ring through?" "Oh yes, it's Bella Brown." Lifting the phone up she says, "I have a Bella Brown here to see Mr Hardcastle." She listens and then puts the phone down. Smiling at me she says, "Miss Bailey, Mr Hardcastle's secretary will be down shortly. Please take a seat." Nodding I sit on the edge of the seat looking around me. I feel as though I have been summoned to the Headmaster's office and don't know why but feel that something bad is about to happen.

About ten minutes later a very glamorous lady comes towards me, her hand outstretched and smiling. She looks to be in her early thirties and is slim with a blonde bob and is very smartly dressed in a black dress and matching jacket. "You must be Bella, hi my name is Amanda, and I am Ben's secretary. I am so pleased to meet you at last." Ordinarily I would be really put out that Ben's secretary is so stunning but she is so friendly that I can't help but warm to her. I notice the receptionist looking at us with curiosity as I follow her to the nearest lift. Once we are inside she says, "I am sorry but Ben is currently in a meeting. You may have to wait a bit but I can get you a cup of

tea or coffee whilst you wait."

"Oh that's ok," I say, "I don't need a drink. I'll just wait until he is free." She leads me to another office which is quite large and I take a seat whilst I wait. I can see a door leading to another office which I assume to be Ben's. Amanda carries on with her work and it must be about ten minutes later when the door opens and a man comes out. He sees me sitting there and looks at me with interest. I smile at him and he says, "Good afternoon."

As he leaves, Amanda looks up and says smiling, "You can go in now Bella."

I go towards the door and don't know why I feel so nervous. As I push it open I can see Ben sitting at his desk with lots of papers all over it and a large computer screen. He looks tired and weary and as he looks up he doesn't smile like he usually does. I smile nervously and say, "Is everything ok?" He just says in a tense voice, "Come in and close the door Bella." I do as he says and say, "What is it Ben? You're making me nervous." He remains seated and fixes me with a penetrating gaze saying, "Do you have anything to feel nervous about?" I swallow hard thinking of the letters and nod. I can hear his sharp intake of breath and looking up I can see that his eyes have darkened in anger. He pulls out a large brown envelope from his desk and takes out some photographs and lays them out on his desk. "Come here Bella and explain these to me," he says angrily. In confusion I go over and am shocked to see that they are pictures of me with Nathan. They were taken the day that I met him at the deli and they are very compromising indeed. There are some taken through the window showing us sitting there. They don't show my face but he is looking lovingly at me and holding my hands. There are a few outside apparently showing us kissing, it looks like I am a willing participant and they don't show the subsequent slap. I look at Ben in horror and my eyes fill up with tears at the look of disappointment in his face. I shake my head saying, "These pictures are not what they look like." He sighs and says, "Tell me then. When were they taken and why didn't you tell me that you had met him?" My head is spinning and I tell him the whole story. I can see that he relaxes slightly and I say, "I am sorry that I didn't tell you. Everything was going wrong for you and I thought that I could handle it. The trouble was it all got on top of me which is why I probably broke down that night. I know I should have told you but I wanted to save you from any more worry." He sighs and takes my hands in his. "How many more times must I tell you Bella? You can trust me and need to tell me everything." Guiltily I think of the letters and I pull away. I go silently to my bag and take them all out. Seeing him look at me with surprise I give them to him and say, "I was also keeping this from you. I was going to tell you last night but you were so stressed out I couldn't bring myself to add to your burden." I watch as he reads them and then anger and disbelief flash across his face. He looks at me with the darkest expression that I have ever seen on his face and he pulls me towards him roughly and hugs me so tightly that I think I may not be able to breathe. He strokes the back of my hair and says with emotion, "I am so sorry Bella. No wonder you have been so upset. Whoever is doing this is trying to break us up. Please don't worry, I will sort it. Just tell me everything, no matter how small it may seem." He sits in his chair and pulls me on to his lap, holding me tightly. We look at the pictures and letters laid out on the desk and I say softly, "It must be Nathan, who else could it be?" He thinks for a moment and says, "He can't have taken the picture of the two of you. If it is him then he has someone helping him." A feeling of dread forms in the pit of my stomach at the thought that there are two people out there trying to split us up. "I don't understand. Why would they go to these extremes? Nathan can't really believe that this would work." Ben's expression is grim and he lifts up his phone and says, "Amanda, get Pete back here please." He puts the phone down and says in a harsh voice. "It bothers me that whoever it is has also been to the house. I don't like the thought of you there on your own if there is somebody out there who is targeting us." Chills run down my spine at his words. I hadn't thought of it like that and I suddenly feel afraid. Sensing this Ben kisses me lightly on the head and says, "Don't worry; I will make sure that you are safe." Looking at the picture of Ben with the woman I say, "Who is this woman Ben, it was taken yesterday wasn't it?" I look at him to see his reaction. His face tenses and his eyes flash. "She is someone I work with. She came to the house because I was working from home. I have known her for years and that is it, just a colleague, certainly not more as this picture suggests."

I believe him, after all my picture looks much more compromising than his, and it is obvious that they are

meant to tell a different story to the one that they actually do. There is a knock on the door and I jump off of Ben's lap feeling embarrassed. Ben grins wickedly at me and pulls me back to sit on him and then says, "Come in." Pete enters the room and looks with surprise at us sitting there. I blush and Ben laughs. "Sorry Pete, I can't stop myself from embarrassing Bella." Pete raises his eyes up and says, "What is it?" Ben's expression grows more serious and he indicates the pictures and letters. Pete comes around the desk to look and his eyes widen and he blows out a big breath. "Well, this is a turn up for the books," he says grimly. Ben nods and I make my escape and go to sit on the chair on the other side of the desk. Pete picks them all up and studies them. Ben looks at him and says, "Can you deal with it?"
Pete nods and gathers them all up. Turning to me he says, "I notice that the envelopes have stamps on them except for this one." I nod and he says, "It must have been pushed through the letter box last night or somebody put it there this morning. It may be a member of staff or someone with access to the building. I will study the CCTV footage at Kinghams and get back to you. Leave it with me Ben; I'll get right on to it." Then he hesitates and looks at me before saying to Ben, "What about the one of you? We need to…" Before he says any more Ben interrupts him and says, "I know. I'll deal with it." Pete looks at me and says, "Bella, if you get anymore let Ben know immediately. If you see or hear anything out of the ordinary let him know." He gives me his card and

says, "Here's my number. Call me if you need anything, night or day." I nod and smile weakly at him. Then Ben says, "You had better sort out the security at the house too. They obviously know where we live and I wouldn't put it past them to come back." Pete nods and then throws me a reassuring smile. "Don't worry Bella. It looks and sounds worse than it is." I smile at him weakly as he leaves the office. Ben stands up and comes over. Pulling me up he holds me against him and I am happy to feel his arms holding me tightly. Tilting my head back he holds my chin and kisses me. Pulling away he studies my face intently and I notice how dark his eyes have gone. I reach up and trace the contours of his face. "I'm sorry that I didn't tell you Ben." I say quietly. His face softens and he says, "I don't blame you Bella. I know your reasons and I love you for them. Don't ever worry about piling pressure on to me, I have broad shoulders and can bear more than you think."

He then lightens his tone and says, "It's good that you're here anyway. It saves me from calling you. I wanted to tell you that we have an Industry awards dinner to attend tonight so you will need to buy a dress for the occasion." He laughs as he watches my reaction. I am amazed and say, "That's a bit short notice don't you think?" Grinning he says, "I wasn't going to go but after the day we've had I think we need to focus on something else for a change. Anyway, I need about an hour to tie things up here which should give you plenty of time to go downstairs

and find a dress. Call me when you're finished and I'll take you to lunch."
Once again I am flabbergasted and say, "But what about work? I can't just take the afternoon off." He fixes me with a wicked smile and says, "I've cleared it with your boss. He will be extremely angry if you don't." Laughing happily I blow him a kiss as I leave the office.

Chapter 13

As I go in search of a dress I think about what has just happened. Things are more serious than I first thought and I just can't shake off the feeling that Ben is keeping something from me that concerns me. Whatever it is that he is trying to protect me from doesn't just affect me, that much is obvious. My mind goes into overdrive but I cannot connect any of the pieces. Pete appeared to know much more than he was saying and I wonder if there is more that I don't know about.

Soon I reach the fashion floor. The brands that are on offer here are high end and even with my staff discount I am going to be hard pushed to find anything in my price range. I look amongst the gorgeous dresses with envy. There is something here to suit most people and I pick up a fabulous red chiffon floor length evening gown. As I hold it against me I can see that it would suit me perfectly. The price ticket shows that it is £690. Sighing I put it back and look around to see if there are any cheaper brands on offer. As I wander around it becomes evident that I am not going to find anything here to suit my budget. I wonder if I have time to go outside and find another more suitable shop on the High street. Looking at my watch I can see that I have about 30 minutes. Heading off outside I look around to see if I can spot a likely shop. There is a small boutique opposite that looks a likely alternative and as I push open the door I am amazed at the amount of choice on offer. Picking up a similar dress to the one I saw opposite I notice that it is £150. The quality is nowhere near as good and it is still a little over my price range. My phone buzzes and I can see that it is Ben calling me. Putting the dress down I say, "Hi Ben, are you done?"

"Yes, where are you and I'll come down?"

"Oh, I've had to go outside; I'll make my way back to meet you at your office if you want?" I can hear his tone change to surprise as he says, "Why are you outside. I thought that you were choosing a dress?" Laughing I say, "I was, but your prices are beyond me I'm afraid so I had to look elsewhere." There is silence and I wonder if the line has gone. Then he says softly, "Meet me by the lifts on the fashion floor."

"Ok, see you in 5 minutes." Smiling at the sales person I head back outside and make my way to the store. As I exit the lift I see Ben waiting for me. He smiles sexily at me and I wonder if I could drag him back into the lift with me. He sees my expression and laughs wickedly. Grabbing my hand he pulls me over to him and says, "Right then, you need a dress. Come and show me the ones that you looked at earlier." Shaking my head I say, "Sorry, they are too expensive. There is one opposite that I could stretch to but it may be better for me to go home and change." He looks at me a smile playing on his lips and says, "What is the point of me owning all of these stores if I can't treat my girlfriend to a dress?" I look at him in surprise and say, "But it's such a waste. I don't want you to waste your money on me." He laughs and says, "Come on. I'm not taking no for an answer and any money I spend on you is not a waste. I am sorry I didn't think when I told you to choose a dress. I should have told you to charge it to my account."

I take him to the red dress and he says, "Go and try it on." I head off to the changing rooms and feel like a princess when I pull the dress on. I can see why it is so expensive. It hugs the contours of my body like a glove and I feel like a million dollars in it. I go outside to get Ben's opinion and he just stares at me, his eyes drawing me in. Coming over he leans towards me and whispers, "You look amazing Bella. I am tempted to come in there with you and help you out of it myself." Laughing I push him away and he says, "Ok, have it your way. Go and get changed and if you want it we'll go and pay for it." As I change I feel a bit guilty. Nobody has ever spent so much money on a dress for me before and it doesn't feel right.

Once I have changed he leads me over to pay. I notice the sales assistant's eyes widen as she sees who her customer is and I can tell that she is on edge. He says, "Please can you pack this dress up and take it to my office. You can ask Miss Bailey to charge it to my account." Nervously the sales assistant says, "Of course Mr Hardcastle, right away." She then looks at me with curiosity and I smile at her to put her at ease. Lowering her eyes she sets about her task and Ben takes my hand and says, "Come on Bella, I'm taking you to lunch." He then proceeds to lead me through the store much to the surprise of the staff. He doesn't let go of my hand and my face flushes at the curious stares of his employees.

Chapter 14

We find a nice little café in which to have our lunch. Sitting tucked away in a corner we snuggle up together on a bench.
I choose a pasta dish and Ben decides on a sandwich with fries. Laughing at him I say, "Do you remember the staff canteen at Cunninghams? We always had burger and chips every Saturday without fail. We were such creatures of habit then." He grins and says, "We've come a long way since then, but our tastes have remained the same." He runs his hands up my leg and flashes me a wicked smile. Arching my eyebrows I say, "If I remember rightly, this wasn't on the menu back then." He smiles ruefully and says, "I couldn't get the courage to ask you out back then. Teasing you was my way of telling you that I liked you." I laugh out loud and say, "Well it didn't work then did it? I never knew that you fancied me. Even at the party I was just one of many that night." He looks at me and his face is full of regret.
"That night I had made up my mind to ask you out. The trouble was I kept on drinking to get the courage. You turned up late and I am afraid I was wasted. When you left I realised that I had ruined everything. From then on I vowed never to lose control again. It had cost me what I wanted the most." Looking at him in surprise I suddenly understand why he has such

control issues. I would never have believed that it was down to me and I feel regret for all of those wasted years.

"Our lives could have been so different," I say, looking at him sadly. Shaking his head he says, "No this was how it was meant to be. It made us who we are today and now that I have found you my life is complete." Tears come in to my eyes and noticing them he hugs me to him. "I love you Bella. I am happy that I found you again. Nothing will ever come between us again." Nodding I snuggle into him. He is my destiny, he always was.

His phone rings and frowning he answers it.

"What have you found?" Listening his face turns serious and he says, "We'll be ten minutes." He looks at me with a grim expression and says, "That was Pete, we need to meet him at my office, he has found something out." Alarm runs through me and quickly we pay and then race back to the store. We are soon in Ben's office where Pete is waiting. As soon as we are inside Ben looks at him questioningly. Pete lays out some images that look as though they are from the CCTV camera. He smiles reassuringly and says, "These are the images taken last night at about 3am." I look at them with interest but all I can make out is a shadowy figure, their face is obscured as they have a large coat on with a hood that hides their features. The other photo shows the image magnified but again it is impossible to tell who it is. Ben studies it for some time, and then he says, "Well it's not Nathan, that much I can tell." Pete nods and says, "I think it is a woman due to their build. I have checked through several hours of footage but this is the only one. I know that this is our letter though because you can clearly see them holding it and posting it through the letterbox." Ben is thoughtful and says, "It may not be an employee then." Pete shrugs and says, "It still may

be. It is obvious that they wanted the letter to get to you today Bella, otherwise they would have posted it like all the others. It could be that they are off today, or work in another store. We certainly can't rule anything out at the moment." He looks grim and says, "I am sorry that this is not more conclusive evidence. I will keep on digging and we are in the process of erecting security cameras and an alarm at the house. I will keep you informed and if you hear or think of anything let me know straight away." We both nod and Pete gathers up his evidence and leaves us to it. Ben looks at me and I can see the strain is showing on his face. Giving me a small smile he says, "Come on, I'm taking you home. We can get ready for the Awards Dinner and try to put this behind us for now."
He tells Amanda what we are doing and we head off home, both of us distracted by our own thoughts.

When we arrive at the house we are greeted by the sight of various workmen installing the security system. I am surprised and say, "How did they get in?" Ben smiles and says, "Mrs Harrison must have been called." Of course, I have only met her a couple of times but I really like Mrs Harrison. She is a local lady who is also a key holder. She cleans twice a week for us and seems to know everything that is going on in the neighbourhood. I know that she has two children who attend the local school and she is active in various community groups, so is the perfect person to ask about anything that is going on.

As we go in she greets us smiling. "Ben, Bella, how nice to see you. Come in I have made a pot of tea for the workmen. Let me get you both a cup." Ben smiles at her gratefully and I say, "Thanks Mrs Harrison. You must have been put out to have to get here so quickly." She shakes her head saying, "Nonsense Bella and please call me Irene. I was only baking at home, which reminds me I brought you some fruit cake, would you like some now?" We both grin at her and say at the same time, "Yes please." She laughs and we follow her into the kitchen. We listen to her chatter for a while and then she says, "Well I had better be off. Just let me know any new instructions for the alarm, otherwise I will be in on Monday as usual." We thank her and I see her out. When I get back to the kitchen Ben says, "You go and get ready Bella. We have to leave at 6pm so we only have a couple of hours. I will sort things out down here as it won't take me as long as you." He raises his eyes up and I pretend to hit him. He grabs my hands and pulls me roughly to him. "Alternatively, I could spend the time sorting you out," he says and then kisses me passionately. I feel the familiar excitement building in my body, and then he reluctantly pulls away as we hear one of the workmen calling for him. Grinning ruefully he releases me and says, "You have been spared this time, but nothing can save you later." He laughs as he sees my expression; obviously I look like someone who didn't want rescuing. I blush and race off upstairs to get ready.

Chapter 15

The Awards dinner is being held at a top London Hotel. We got here at 7pm and it is due to start at 7.30pm. The Hardcastle group has a table for the event which is made up of various managers from the stores and their wives or girlfriends. Ben looks absolutely gorgeous in a black dinner suit and I feel amazing in my new dress. We get some interested looks as we arrive at the table and I remember that this is the first time that I have met Ben's management team. They all seem pleasant and I take my seat next to the manager of the Kingston store and his wife. Ben is on my other side and I look with interest around me. The room is made up of various other retail sectors and there are hundreds of people here, all dressed up and looking amazing. There is a stage that has a podium and a microphone set up on it, with the graphics behind of the awards ceremony logo. All of the awards are set up on a table nearby and a well known comedian is due to act as the compere.

We are served wine and offered other drinks and soon our starter arrives. I chat happily to Mark and Lesley, next to me and discover that we have a lot in common. Ben appears quite relaxed and I am glad to see that the rest of his team appear relaxed in his company. Laughing to myself I realise that this is the first time that I have seen people who are actually relaxed around him.

The evening goes on and once we have eaten the awards ceremony begins. I can see why they need a comedian to officiate as it could otherwise be extremely dull.

The nominees are read out and then the comedian announces the winner. It appears endless and I find myself drinking far too much. Hardcastles wins a couple of awards, Best group of stores and Best promotion campaign. Two of the store managers go up to receive them and I whisper to Ben, "Why don't you go up and collect any?" He grimaces and says, "No thanks. It's not my thing. I never normally come as things like this don't interest me. I would prefer the people who are actually responsible to receive the recognition." I smile at him and squeeze his hand. Squeezing mine back he whispers, "I would rather be at home with you. The way you are looking in that dress makes me want to ditch this and go and book us a room instead." I blush again and seeing him laugh I feel furious with myself. I push my chair back saying, "Sorry call of nature. I won't be long." He grins and turns his attention back to the ceremony.

I walk outside to find the Ladies and locate it not far from the room. It is a relief in more ways than one as I have been sitting for so long at the table.

When I exit the cubicle I notice a lady standing at the basin washing her hands. As she looks at me she looks familiar but I can't quite place her. She smiles at me and then realisation hits me, this is the lady from the photograph at the house. Shock must have registered on my face because she nods and then says, "Hello Bella. I can tell that you recognise me which makes this easier. We haven't got long before Ben will become suspicious so please hear me out." I feel amazed and just stare at her, wondering what she wants. She continues.

"Nobody will come in as I have put a closed sign on the door. Just tell Ben that you had to go off in search of another toilet which is why you were so long. Now as I said I haven't got much time so any questions please keep until the end." She looks at me with a hard expression and says, "I need to trust you Bella to say nothing of our conversation to anyone especially Ben. When I have finished I am sure that you will understand why." I feel extremely curious which is a good thing; otherwise I would be tempted to race out of there.

She carries on. "Ben has worked for me for a number of years now. We work for the government and are responsible for infiltrating organisations that pose a threat to our way of life." I feel a huge amount of shock at her words and try not to let it show on my face. She is studying me intently and carries on speaking.

"We have been monitoring Nathan Matthews for nearly two years now and have discovered that he has been obtaining information on financial accounts from various organisations and businesses." This is now too much and I sink into a nearby chair. I can't believe that Nathan is a criminal.

"Bella, I know this is a shock but you must hear me out. I haven't got long." I nod and she says, "The cyber attack on the stores was just a petty distraction. He has bigger fish to fry and was using his position at Kinghams as a cover. We have found out most of what we need to know but there is still vital evidence missing. When you left him it became apparent that he was desperate. We are not sure but think that you hold the key to this missing information, although we are aware of your innocence in this. We have planted an operative close to him and she has discovered that he is compiling a list of codes. We believe that they are the information that he needs to collate to put his plan into action. He needs all of them for his system to work and we think that he has scattered them over several places as an insurance policy in case he was caught. Without them all his plan cannot progress." I am now totally lost and look at her in consternation. She quickly carries on saying, "We think that he has planted some of the codes on you or your family. When you left him he no longer had access to them and needs to retrieve them. He is now desperate to get you back and will stop at nothing to achieve this. The letters and the orchestrated photographs are just the beginning. He is also not working alone and we believe that a Bradley Summers is his accomplice." My mind is reeling. I think of Tina and wonder if she knows any of this. "What we need Bella, is for you to go back to Nathan. Ben has told us that it is not an option and is not moving on it. It was inconvenient that you had history and that he loves you. It is holding up the operation and we cannot convince him. The only way that we can resolve this and move on is for you to go back and for him to finish what he started. We will monitor you closely but I must make you aware that there are risks. Nathan is not the gentle soul that you think he is and if he discovers that you know anything you may be in danger. It is why Ben wants to protect you and he mustn't know of our plan."

My eyes fill with tears as her words sink in. Turning to look at her I say, "But how can I go back to Nathan and convince Ben at the same time that I am leaving him?" As I say the words a sob escapes from my throat and my heart clenches in anguish. Ben's boss looks at me with a hard expression. "We will present the opportunity to you. You will know when the time is right. I need you to say that you will help us because Nathan will not stop until he has you back and all the time you delay it could spell danger for Ben. The fact that he has now seen Ben and I together may risk the operation. Nathan may dig deeper and our cover could be blown. In doing this you are doing the right thing for your country and the man you love."

I realise that she is right. I need to end this. Even if it means that I lose Ben in the process. I need to protect him as he is doing for me and it will be the hardest thing that I have ever had to do.

Looking up at her hard face I nod silently. She lets out a breath and says, "You are doing the right thing Bella. Now go back and don't let Ben know that anything has happened. He mustn't know and must believe that you are leaving him. I will arrange for the opportunity to present itself. I will contact you soon with further instructions. Now go because I understand that he is becoming unsettled." Looking at her in surprise I notice that she is wearing an ear piece. I jump up and as I pass her she looks at me and for a second her features soften, "Thank you Bella. I know that this is hard for you. You are doing the right thing though." Looking away I head back to the ceremony with a very heavy heart, Why don't I feel as though I am?

Chapter 16

As I walk back I try to take everything in. I can't believe it. I would never have thought that Nathan was a criminal mastermind. I would have been less surprised if she had told me it was Ben. Thinking of him tears come into my eyes. I don't know how I am going to do this. The thought of leaving him is too much to bear. He will believe that I am going back to Nathan voluntarily. If I don't do it though he could be harmed and I couldn't bear that.

I push open the door and a sharp pain shoots through me as I see him sitting at the table. Mustering all of my strength I approach the table. He smiles at me and my heart breaks in two. I see his eyes narrow and as I sit down he leans towards me. "What's wrong Bella?" he says his eyes burning into mine. Falteringly I hold my hand up to my head and say, "I'm sorry but I have a raging headache that came on suddenly." Seeing the look of concern on his face tears spring into my eyes. Grabbing my hand he says, "Come on. I'm taking you home." Shaking my head I say, "We can't leave, it would be rude." "I don't care, you come first and if you're not well then we won't stay here a minute more than necessary." As he whispers his goodbyes to the others I feel wretched. Everyone looks at me with concern and I feel a total fraud. Ben takes my hand and we leave. I feel as though I have drifted into a nightmare and I can't see any way out of it.

As soon as we get home Ben orders me up to bed and says that he will bring me some tea up. As I run a bath I choke back the tears. I look around me at the place I now call home. I am so happy with Ben and the thought that I will have to devastate him to save him is too much to bear. Lying in the bath my mind spins around with everything that I have learnt. Ben brings me some painkillers and a cup of tea and I can't help the tears that begin to fall. He crouches down next to me and strokes my hair which makes me cry even more. "What is it Bella, is it the headache or is there something else bothering you?" He is looking at me with such love that it is unbearable. I try to get myself together, if I don't he will guess, so I say, "I'm so sorry Ben. I feel upset that I ruined our evening. I don't often get headaches this bad but for some reason this one tonight is unbearable. I suppose I am crying because I ruined your night and I feel so ill." His eyes soften and he kisses my fingers. "Don't be silly Bella. I wasn't bothered about the awards ceremony. You are the only thing that matters to me. Come on out you get and off to bed. You can sleep it off and no work for you tomorrow." I do as he says, desperate to close my eyes and try to shut out the nightmare that I am now in.

Ben makes sure that I am tucked up and have everything that I need and then leaves me to it. Lying in the darkness I think about what is to come. It all seems so unbelievable and I am not sure if I will be able to pull it off. One thing is for sure though, Ben mustn't guess a thing, he would stop me in an instant and then we would be in danger.

The next morning I sleep in. Ben has already left for work but he left a note for me to call him when I wake up. He answers immediately. "Hi Bella, how are you feeling?" he says in a gentle voice. Fighting back the tears once again I say, "Much better thank you. Did you get much sleep yourself last night?" He laughs guiltily and says, "I didn't want to disturb you so I

worked a lot of it." Feeling bad I say, "You are in so much trouble."

There is a long pause and then he replies, "Well maybe if you're up to it you can punish me later." In spite of myself I laugh softly. "If you can take it then I might just do that." I hear his breath draw in and then he says, "I'm on my way." The phone cuts off and I smile to myself. I will never get enough of him, but then the pain hits me and I remember that I will have to make the most of the time that we do still have because one thing is for sure, they won't hang around. Within the hour I hear his car in the drive. The door slams and I hear him run upstairs. As he bursts into the room I laugh at his determined expression. His eyes are full of lust and excitement runs through me. This is going to take some time. Slowly he approaches the bed, his gaze holding me and his dark eyes drawing me in. I watch as he rips off his tie, followed by his suit. Soon he is naked before me and I give him a seductive look and lick my lips in anticipation. He moves towards me slowly as though stalking his prey and I lean back on to the bed, the straps of my satin nightdress falling to the side. I start to quiver at the thought of what is to come. He sits on the edge of the bed and pulls me towards him, holding my hair in place securely and kissing me with such passion that I almost can't breathe. He leans me back and then proceeds to make love to me with so much love and passion that I almost cry at how it makes me feel. I am not even sure how long we stay in bed. Every time I think that we have finished he does something else to excite me again. I have never experienced such sensuality. He has taken me to places that I never thought possible before. Today we are at another level, it is almost as though we both know that things are about to change and need to make the most of each other for the short time that we have left.

Chapter 17

It is about a week later and nothing has yet happened. I have received three more letters which I duly gave to Ben. Each one was worse than the preceding one and I now just feel numb to them. Phoebe and Boris have invited us out for a meal and I am looking forward to meeting up with them. I need the distraction as I am constantly on edge, wondering when Ben's boss is going to show her hand.

We meet them outside a favourite restaurant of Phoebes. "Bella, Ben!" she cries, running towards us as we approach and hugs us both. "Come on I'm freezing." I laugh and say, "Well you could have waited inside; in fact I am amazed that you didn't. You would normally have ordered a bottle of wine by now." She pouts and says, "The table wasn't ready and Boris had to make a phone call, so I waited outside with him." We all laugh and make our way inside. Once we have ordered, Phoebe turns to us her eyes shining. "Guess what?" We shake our heads and she says, "Our house has completed and we move on the 20th. What do you think about that?" We grin at her excitement and congratulate them. For a moment my heart sinks as I remember that I won't be living nearby for much longer. I push the sadness away. I can't dwell on it. I must be strong and then we can put all of this behind us. I have to cling on to the hope that once this is all over Ben will forgive me. If I don't have hope then I know that I won't go through with it. We have a lovely meal and drink far too much wine. Before long it is time to go and we get up to leave. Ben holds the door open and we all go outside. Turning I hug Phoebe and Boris goodbye. As I pull away I suddenly notice that the conversation has stopped. Their expressions are ones of shock and looking at Ben I can see that he has gone pale. My heart plummets and even before I turn around I know that this is it.

Slowly I turn around and see Nathan standing there looking at us with a serious expression. He is not alone and I am shocked to see none other than Melissa standing next to him. I look at Ben and see that his face is full of anger. His eyes have darkened and I start to tremble as I see the menace in his eyes. However it is not Nathan at whom it is directed but Melissa. I can see that she is uncomfortable and is looking very pale and frightened. Nathan steps forward and says, "I am sorry to break up this happy gathering but I have something to tell Bella that I think she should know." Phoebe is looking at me with concern and Boris looks uncomfortable. Melissa is looking at Ben and I can see the resignation in her face. I have never seen Ben look so angry and as I look at Nathan I notice that he is looking at Ben with a triumphant expression. Nathan steps towards me and his face softens. "I am sorry to do this to you Bella but you have to know the truth. Melissa contacted me as she has been struggling with what she did to you and came to me to put things right." He flashes a brief look of dislike towards Ben and then carries on. "Melissa was never Ben's girlfriend." I can hear the gasp of shock from Phoebe but I don't turn around. I keep on staring at Nathan knowing what he is about to say. "Ben hired her to split us up. He wanted you and was going to stop at nothing to get you. The weekend away was always designed to achieve that aim. Melissa was to seduce me and then carry on seeing me behind your back. The pregnancy was a lie designed to put the final nail in the coffin." I look at Nathan, my eyes filling with tears. Moving towards me he is standing just an arms length away. I can feel Ben's eyes boring into me but I can't look at him. Nathan says gently, "We never stood a chance baby. I always knew that something had happened but I didn't know for sure until Melissa called me and confessed. I had to let you know the truth. The man you are with is a fraud and a manipulator. You deserve better than that." I look over at Melissa and tears run down her cheeks. She says in a faltering voice, "Please forgive me Bella. I only did it for the money, I never thought that it would matter to me but I grew to like you and Nathan and the longer I lived with the secret the harder it became." I notice that she won't look at Ben and I try to muster every ounce of resolve to see this through. Tears run down my face. Not for the reasons that they all think, but because of what I have to do next.

I slowly turn to face Ben and look towards him with a stricken expression. He moves towards me and I can see the pain in his eyes. He speaks in a low husky voice. "Bella please, don't listen to them. You know that I would never do anything to hurt you, quite the contrary. You are the most important thing in my life and I love you more than you will ever know." I can't stop the tears that fall, my hurt and anguish very much coming to the fore. I know that what I say next is more for Nathan's benefit than anyone else's and I steel myself to deliver the blows that I know I have to. Looking at Ben I say in an emotional voice, "Enough Ben, I can't take it anymore. Everybody warned me about you but I thought I knew better. How many more times am I going to hear what you have supposedly done? I thought that I knew you but it turns out that I knew nothing. You knew that I was engaged and happy with Nathan, but you had to ruin it didn't you?" Panic and disbelief flashes into his eyes and at the sight of it the tears come much quicker. He makes as if to take my hand and I move away from him sharply, the very act of which shatters my heart. I cannot bear the look of desperation and anguish in his face and want to get as far away from everyone as I can. The trouble is I can't bear what I am doing to him. Raising my eyes to his I look at him with a look that I hope he understands. I need him to let this go and leave me to do what I have to do. I cannot have him trying to interfere and as he sees my expression he takes a physical step back in shock. I am looking at him how he looks at me. I am willing him to trust me and I put everything into my eyes. I know that he understands. I can see the shock and realisation setting in and I know that he has understood. He cannot change this; he has to release me so that I can end this.

I turn towards Nathan and Melissa and say, "Well you've got what you came for. I am finished with this."

Turning to Phoebe I say in a faltering voice, "Please can I come home with you Phoebs?" She rushes over and puts her arm around me, looking at the other three with dislike. "Come on Bella, we'll look after you." We walk away and my heart is left behind. I have never felt such desolation and I just want to get as far away from all of them as I can.

Chapter 18

I go back to the flat, as I have done so many times before. It no longer feels like home though and I realise that I no longer have one. Phoebe sat next to me the whole way back and comforted me.
As soon as we get back Boris makes us all a drink and then leaves us alone. Phoebe hugs me and says, "Oh Bella, I am so sorry. I know what Nathan said but I do feel that Ben loves you more than anything. It is unforgivable what he did though and poor Nathan." I don't want to hear any sympathy for Nathan but know that I can't say anything. I just nod and let myself adjust to the situation. I don't even know what the next step will be but I know that life is not going to be easy. We must sit there for hours. Phoebe doesn't pry or push me which I am grateful for.
Much later we decide to go to bed although I am not sure how much sleep I will get. I lie in my old room that was once so familiar to me but now feels strange. The bed feels empty without Ben in it and there is a hole where my heart used to be. I feel numb and I worry about how Ben is feeling now. The thought of what I have to do fills me with dread. I know that the plan will be to let Nathan back into my life. I will have to be strong and try to end this swiftly.
I do not sleep at all and just take comfort in the darkness. It must be about 6am when the phone that

Ben bought me rings. Looking at it with alarm I notice a strange number. I answer it in a low voice and am not surprised to hear Ben's boss on the other end. "Well done Bella, you have done the right thing. Now hear me out and do not speak at all," she says briskly and professionally. I know that this is common place and just business to her and I feel the anger mounting in me. "I won't be calling you again so listen carefully. We will arrange for your things to be returned to you from Ben's house. There will be some tracking devices and monitoring equipment disguised in some items. You will not know what they are but rest assured we will be keeping a close eye on you. Nathan must not think that anything is wrong. We need you to start seeing him again and to give him access to your property as he would have before. Keep an eye on him for anything out of the ordinary. He will be looking to retrieve the codes that he has secreted on your possessions and as soon as he has them he will make his move. You don't need to do anything at all just play along. We have arranged for an initial two week absence from work at full pay so that you can avoid any confrontations with Ben. He is not happy and has of course realised what we did. Do not have any contact with him at all and under no circumstances try to do any of your own investigations. You may be in considerable danger if he realises what you are up to. Once again thank you for your help with this and good luck." The phone goes dead and I realise that not only has she ended the call but the phone has been disconnected. The tears flow freely again. This was my contact with Ben. He wouldn't be able to contact me at all or I him. The thought of what he must be going through is too much to think about. He is always so in control, it will be destroying him.

I must have lay there thinking for a couple of hours before Phoebe knocks on my door. She peers around the door and says, "Morning Bella, I've brought you a cup of tea. Did you manage to get any sleep?" I shake my head and she comes and sits on the bed.

"I can't believe that happened last night," she says with concern. I give her a small smile and say, "I'm sorry that you and Boris got caught up in it all." Grabbing hold of my hand she says, "Don't be silly. I am glad that we were there. You need your friends at times like this. Don't worry about anything. You can stay here for as long as you like." I smile gratefully and once again the tears that are never far away spill down my cheeks. Phoebe grabs me a tissue from the bedside table and gives me a hug. "Let it all out Bella. Don't hold back. You will feel better for it." She climbs into bed with me and puts her arm around my shoulders, just sitting with me silently whilst I let it all out.

Much later I start to feel better. I try to channel my thoughts into other things and think of the practicalities of my situation. Ben's boss had said that my stuff would be packed up and sent to me and that I was to be off work for two weeks. Phoebe said earlier that I could move back in if necessary and so it will be like old times - almost.

I wonder how long it will be before I hear from Nathan. In a way I hope that it is soon. I just want to get this all over with, although I am worried at how I will act with him given what I now know. Phoebe has lent me some clothes but I know that I will need my things soon.

I needn't have worried though. Phoebe sent Boris to Ben's house to get some of my things. He brings them in and throws me a worried smile. I ask, "Did you see Ben, how was he?" Boris looks down and says, "Not good I'm afraid. He was more concerned about how you were but I could see that he hadn't slept. I know what Nathan said, as well as all of the bad things that I have heard, but I felt sorry for him. I didn't want any of it to be true." He looks so upset that I run over and give him a massive hug. He looks at me in surprise and I say, "Thanks Boris, you're a good friend." Embarrassed he shuffles out of the room and Phoebe raises her eyes. "He's not good at the emotional stuff Bella. He feels bad for you both though. I think he really got to like Ben once he got to know him. We both did." The tears spring up again and I try to get a grip. The phone rings and Phoebe answers it. I see her eyes widen in alarm and I guess that the caller is Nathan. She mouths that it is him and I nod and hold out my hand. He hasn't hung about which I am glad about. Taking the phone I say quietly, "Nathan?" I hear his familiar voice and his tone is soft and gentle. "Hi Bella. I'm sorry to call you so soon but I have been worried about you." I sniff and say, "Well I'm not too good as you probably would expect after last night." There is a short silence and then he says, "Look, take all the time you need but we need to talk. I have so much that I want to say and if you feel up to it we could meet somewhere of your choosing." I can see Phoebe shaking her head and I know that she is concerned about me. With a deep breath I say, "I owe you that at least. I'll meet you in the park in an hour by the café."

I hang up without waiting for a reply. Phoebe looks cross. "Bella, don't meet Nathan, it's too soon. You need to get your head around it all first." Gently I say, "I need to sort it out Phoebs. It will still be there tomorrow and the day after that and the day after that. I am not sure what is going to happen but I need to deal with it now." "Do you want me to come with you?" I shake my head. "No, I'll be fine. It will be good to get some fresh air anyway." She nods and then I set about getting ready for the inevitable.

Chapter 19

I can see him waiting as I approach. I feel nervous to meet him as I am not sure what my reaction will be. Such a lot has happened since we were together and knowing what I now know about him isn't helping. He stands up as he sees me coming and smiles nervously at me. "It's good to see you baby, how are you?" I manage a weak smile and just shrug saying, "Ok, I think." He looks towards the café and says, "Would you like to go inside for a coffee, or would you rather just walk?"

"Can we just walk for now Nathan?" I say quietly, thinking that a walk would help relieve some of the tension, rather than staring at each other over a table. We set off and it is almost like old times, without the closeness that we once shared. He clears his throat and says, "I'm sorry that I had to break it to you like that Bella. It must have been a huge shock but I couldn't let him work out a way to wriggle out of it. He has been lying to you for months." I just nod and he carries on. "Melissa came to me and told me. She was very frightened of confronting the two of you which is why we had to do it in front of witnesses and in the open. She said that he was capable of anything and wouldn't just allow us to walk in there and tear you apart." I try to quell the feeling of rising anger within me as I hear him talk about Ben as though he is a monster. He carries on talking in a gentle voice. "I have known ever since you left me that it didn't all add up. The more I found out about him the worse it got. The stories are just hearsay but there are too many of them for some of it not to be true. I couldn't find out any hard evidence but carried on digging. Then I got arrested and believe that he set me up to stop me digging any further. I tried to get you to see what he was like but he had cast a spell over you and you couldn't see it." A tear escapes and runs down my cheek. Seeing it Nathan stops in alarm. He spins me around to face him and takes me in his arms. "Please don't cry Bella. I can't bear it. All that mattered to me was getting you away from that monster. I love you and always have. I know that I screwed up and have been punishing myself ever since. I am not stupid enough to think that we can go back to how we were but I would like us to be friends, and then who knows, maybe one day you will learn to love me again." The more he says the more I cry. If I didn't know better his speech would have moved me. He was always so eloquent and easy to get on with. It would be easy to go back to him but I know that I have a job to do. The trouble is every word he says is accompanied by a lie. My tears are for what he has become and what I know that I will have to do. I feel numb inside as if part of me is missing, which I know will only be complete again when and if Ben and I are back together.

He looks at me with concern and says, "Come on; let me buy you a coffee. We can talk it all through inside." I allow myself to be guided in to the café and we sit at a table by the window. I remember how we used to meet up for lunch most days and how we used to enjoy spending time together.

As we sit there he says, "What are you going to do about Ben?" Once again tears come into my eyes and I say shakily, "It's over. I am moving back in with Phoebe and Boris. I have taken two weeks off work and have asked him to send over my belongings." He looks taken aback but I can see the relief in his face. Reaching over the table he takes my hand. "I'm sorry that you're hurting Bella. Just know that I am here for you and anything you want at all you can rely on me. Even if it's just for some company."

Mustering a small smile I say, "I know. Thank you for everything Nathan. I am still letting it all sink in and it may take some time, but I value your friendship. I have missed that and am glad that you are here." The words come out of my mouth but I don't mean any of them. I really want to shout and scream at him and tell him what I really think of him but I keep it all inside, buried deep within me. It will come out, but only when the time is right.

We chat generally about our families for a while and I am genuinely interested to hear about them. Despite everything I got on well with them all. I wonder what they will do when the truth comes out. Pushing those thoughts to the back of my mind I stand up and say, "Well I must be going Nathan. Thank you for the coffee and for meeting me. It was good to catch up and even though I am still coming to terms with everything, I am grateful that you cared enough to

show me what Ben is really like."
He looks at me with surprise and I think that he was probably hoping that we would spend longer together. He quickly pushes back his seat and follows me outside. "Let me walk you home Bella."
Shaking my head I try to smile. "No, thank you for offering though. I just need some time on my own if you don't mind." He looks at me with a worried expression and says, "Of course, I understand. Would it be ok to call you tomorrow though?" Nodding I say, "Yes, I would like that Nathan. Thank you again." Then I walk away trying to get as much distance between us as I can.

Chapter 20

Once I get inside the flat I am greeted by boxes and boxes littering the place. Hearing the door Phoebe comes out of the kitchen and throws me a worried look. With a sinking feeling I realise that this is my stuff from Ben's. I can't help myself and burst out crying. Phoebe rushes over and puts her arm around me. "I'm sorry Bella, it arrived an hour ago. It seems so brutal."

I knew that it was coming but I still wasn't prepared for the effect it has on me. It all seems so final and I remember how happy I was when I moved in with Ben. It just isn't fair. We should still be together. I was happier than I had ever been in my life and now I am alone and so is he.

Phoebe pulls me over to the settee and says, "Leave it all for now. I'll get you a drink and when you feel up to it I will help you move it all back into your room."

Sitting here I think how awful it must have been for Ben to sort it all out. I know that this would have been much more of a shock to him. I just hope that he realises why I had to do it. Gingerly I reach out and lift the top of the nearest box open. It looks to be my clothes. With a deep breath I decide to set about unpacking the boxes. The sooner they are sorted the better I will feel. It's not fair on Phoebe or Boris to have them littering the place.

When Phoebe comes back in with the drinks she says nothing and just helps me move the boxes into my room one at a time. Once the last box is in she says, "Would you like a hand with the unpacking?" Shaking my head I say, "I'll be fine. It will give me something to do anyway." Closing the door quietly she leaves me to it and I set about the arduous task. Most of the

boxes contain clothing. The worst thing is when I see the red dress that Ben had bought me. Holding it against me I let myself go. I had been so happy that day until the bombshell at the awards ceremony. The tears just come thick and fast and it is some time before I can carry on.

The rest isn't too bad until I come to the little canvas picture that Ben gave me. This sets me off again and once again I hold it to me. I will never forget the time we spent at the lodge. I wish that I was there now with Ben. Once again we had been so happy there. As I look at it though I notice that something is different about it. It seems bigger than I remember. Turning it over I notice that it has been framed. This is odd. It wasn't framed when I left it. All of a sudden I realise why. Ben's boss had said that they would be watching me. They must have put some sort of device in the frame. Brushing away my tears I stare at the canvas. I imagine that Ben can see me and I reach out and trace the picture gently. I don't speak but my eyes say it all for me. It is as though he is looking at me now. I want him to see that I love him. Having the picture near me is my link with him. Tenderly I put it back up on the

shelf opposite my bed. It will be the first thing I see in the morning and the last thing at night.
Somehow I feel a little better, although I am probably imaging it anyway. The picture however is not the only thing that is different. Tucked away amongst the clothes is a little padded box. As I open it I see the most beautiful
silver pendant. It takes my breath away and once again I cannot stop the tears. The pendant is of two badgers. I put it over my head and hold it close. I know that this is Ben's way of telling me that he still loves me. Just those two things are enough to set my heart to rest and give me the resolve to finish this once and for all.
Phoebe and Boris have organised a takeaway with a film to watch for the evening. I am so grateful to them and we just sit silently watching the film. By the time it has finished I am ready for bed. I am exhausted as I didn't sleep at all last night and thanking them I head off for a bath and bed. I sleep with my pendant on and make sure that the last thing I see is my picture.

When I wake up the next day I can see that I have overslept. It is 10am and then it all comes flooding back to me. I should be going to work today but remember that I have time off. Phoebe and Boris have both gone to work and Phoebe has left me a note to call her to meet up in her lunch hour. I get ready and before I can think what to do next the doorbell rings. As I open it I see Nathan leaning on the doorframe looking at me with the gentle expression that used to give me butterflies. "You look better today baby." He says smiling. My heart sinks but I plaster a smile on my face. "Nathan, come in. Let me get you a drink." He follows me inside and I gesture for him to take a seat. He follows me into the kitchen though and leans against the side watching me. "Shouldn't you be at work?" I say to him in surprise and he replies grinning, "Yes I should actually, but I threw a sickie to come and see you." I look at him and he throws me his cheeky look that I always loved. Seeing him standing here in the kitchen like he used to it is almost as though the last few months haven't happened. As though reading my thoughts he moves over to me and takes my hand. "We should be married now," he says somewhat bitterly. Nodding I give him a rueful smile and say, "I know." Taking my hand away I continue with the drinks. It is obvious that he wants things to get back to how they were. It is probably so that he can gain access to wherever he has hidden the codes, although I do believe that he had loved me before and may still. I hand him his drink and we stand there contemplating each other. After a while he says, "Would you like to go out somewhere Bella? We could grab some lunch at a pub like we used to and keep each other company. You don't have to talk about any of this if you don't want to." Smiling I say, "Ok, I'll just grab my bag, I won't be long." Racing off into the bedroom I decide to take my time. If he needs to look around the flat I want to give him some space to do so. I go into the bathroom and sort out my hair and make up until I think that I have given him long enough. When I get back to the lounge I see that he is studying the books in the bookcase. He smiles as I walk in and says, "I forgot how many good books you have here." Smiling I say, "I'm sure that Phoebs and Boris wouldn't mind if you wanted to borrow one." I look at him with interest, disguising the fact that I am observing which one he picks. He laughs and says, "I wouldn't have time to read them anyway. Despite playing hooky today I am really busy at work." I look at him to see if there is any other sign but all appears normal so I say, "You haven't told me about your new job. What is it that you do?" Smiling he says, "I work with Bradley at an Insurance company. We as you would expect work in the IT department and look after the systems there."

I remember when I met Tina and say, "That's right. When I last saw Tina she mentioned that Bradley was doing really well there and that they were buying a house in Ripley due to the large bonus he received." Nathan looks surprised and says, "I didn't know that you had met up. You're right though. They have moved in now and the house is amazing. I must take you there some time." I don't answer but then say, "Do you have as much opportunity as him to earn good money?" Smiling he says, "Yes, the pay is generous, which is why Bradley kept on at me to join him. I resisted for ages though because I wanted to stay near you." I flush and look away. He moves towards me and says brightly, "Anyway, let's go and eat. I am looking forward to spending some time with my favourite girl."

Chapter 21

On the way to the pub I text Phoebe to say that I can't meet her. I would much rather meet up with her but I have a job to do and I want to finish it as soon as possible.
Nathan is on his full charm offensive and tries to keep the conversation light and humorous. We order our food and find a table. Nathan sits next to me on the bench and his leg rests against mine. I really want to move away but as I am in the corner there is nowhere to go. Trying to ignore it I have a sudden thought. Turning towards him I say, "Are you still going out with Sophie?" He looks surprised and then looks at me a guilty expression on his face. "No, we finished last week. She was nice, but she wasn't you." He then smiles softly at me and his eyes lock on to mine and hold my gaze. I blink to break the connection and say, "I'm sorry. She is nice and I thought that you were both well suited." Smiling briefly he then says, "The trouble is baby, I am in love with you. You have spoilt it for me and anyone else. I kept on comparing her to you in my mind and she didn't measure up." I blush with embarrassment. This I don't want to hear. He looks amused and says, "I intend to fight for you Bella. You may not be ready to take me back now, but I am going to prove to you that we are meant to be together even if it kills me." Luckily I am spared from

answering as our food arrives. As we eat I am conscious of his close proximity to me. I feel trapped in more ways than one and am not sure if I can see it all through.

I try to change the subject on to safer ground and ask him to tell me about his job. He tells me all about it and I listen whilst I eat. Once we have finished he leans back and puts his arm around me. Flinching I try to pull away and I notice that his eyes harden. He keeps it in place and I will myself to relax. Even though I don't want to be close to him, I do understand that a certain amount of contact will be needed for the plan to work. Despite my reservations we do have a nice lunch and Nathan can be so charming when he wants to be. I always enjoyed his company and he talks about things that happened when we were together and I soon find myself laughing at his stories.

We head off back to the flat and when we get to the door he smiles at me and says, "Aren't you going to invite me in for coffee?" He raises his eyes in a suggestive way and I push him jokingly and say, "Just a coffee, nothing else." I hope that if he can relax in the flat he may find what he is looking for. As we go in I say over my shoulder, "Take a seat Nathan and I'll put the kettle on. Turn on the TV if you want." I leave him in the living room and set about making the drinks. I would love to be able to watch him to see what he does but I don't want him to become suspicious. As I go in I see that he is flicking through a magazine. He pats the seat next to him and says,

"Come and sit next to me Bella and I'll tell you your fortune." He indicates the horoscope section in the magazine and laughing I do as he says. He starts to read it out. "Hmm, Pisces. Right - today you will meet up with an old flame who will turn out to be your destiny. Don't fight the inevitable." He smirks at me and I raise my eyes. Grabbing the magazine I say, "Let me read yours, Aries isn't it? Ok - You are heading for a fall, give up on your plans, they make take longer than you first thought and it won't be worth the effort." I look blankly at him and he laughs. He takes the magazine from my hand and then leans towards me until his face is centimetres from mine. I can feel his breath on my face and his eyes hold me as he looks at me with a hard glint in them. He reaches up and runs his fingers around the back of my head. Pulling me towards him he whispers, "I will persevere and I will win in the end. I will never give up on us no matter how long it takes." I blink in confusion and then he releases me and pulls away. He leans back

sipping his coffee and stares long and hard at me. I shift in my seat not really knowing what to say. Suddenly he laughs and says, "Anyway, I have to go now. I have enjoyed today and was hoping that you might like to meet up again tomorrow evening. We could go to the cinema if you like. I know a film that you would like and it would take your mind off

things." Nodding I say, "Ok, where shall I meet you?"
"It's alright I'll pick you up at 7pm."
"Ok, thanks for lunch, I'll see you tomorrow." As soon

as he leaves I close the door and race into my room shutting the door behind me. I look at the canvas and lay on my bed. I picture Ben in my mind. I need to remove Nathan from my thoughts and replace them with Ben. It is the only way that I will survive this.

That evening is spent with Phoebe and Boris. Phoebe was horrified to hear of my lunch with Nathan and even more so when she heard of our date tomorrow night. "What are you thinking Bella? Its way too soon to start seeing Nathan, especially after all that has gone on between you." Boris looks worried and I feel bad. They must think that I am heartless, bouncing between Nathan and Ben like a tennis ball. I just hope that one day they will learn the truth.

Chapter 22

The next day I decide to go and break the news to my parents. They will need to believe that Ben and I have broken up so that I can take Nathan around to the house. It may be that he has stored something there, so the sooner I take him the better.

However I needn't have worried because they already knew. Nathan had obviously told his parents and his mum had duly informed mine. I felt bad as it can't have been nice for her to hear the news second hand. She busies herself making some lunch saying, "I couldn't believe it when Marie told me about Ben. He is so cold. I knew that you should have believed Nathan at Phoebe's wedding. Don't get me wrong I liked him well enough and he seemed to treat you well, but all those things that were said were despicable. Thank goodness that Nathan loves you as much as he does to rescue you." I let her whittle on but I tune out. I can't sit and listen to her bad mouthing Ben. If only she knew the real truth then she would be singing a different tune. She finishes by saying, "Well you must invite Nathan for Sunday lunch so that we can say thank you. It's the least we can do." Nodding I say, "Ok, I'll ask him." She looks at me and I can see the excitement in her eyes. She is obviously hoping for a reconciliation between us and my heart sinks as I know that she is going to be well and truly shocked when the truth eventually comes out.

Later that evening Nathan comes as agreed at 7pm. I try to ignore Phoebe's disapproving looks and make a quick exit. Nathan takes my arm and leads me down to his car. I look at it in surprise as I was expecting his usual Golf. He now has a new Porsche and it looks amazing. I turn and look at him in amazement and he laughs and says, "Moved on a bit since Kinghams haven't I?" Shaking my head I say, "You are obviously getting paid well." Grinning at me he says, "This is just the tip of the iceberg baby. Stay with me and you'll be set for life." I sit in the passenger seat feeling very uncomfortable. He is obviously setting his plan into motion and the job is probably just a cover story. I try to look impressed and he enjoys showing the car off to me. It doesn't take us long and we are soon at the cinema. We grab some drinks and popcorn and I follow him into a vacant row. There are not many people in the theatre and the film soon starts. I am glad that we are seeing a film because then I don't have to make conversation with him. I know that all of this is necessary, we need to be at least friends again for him to gain access to the places that he may have stored the codes. Anything other than friendship is most definitely off the cards but I know that I will have my work cut out keeping him at arms length. After the film he suggests going to the local Chinese restaurant for dinner. I accept but am getting weary with all of the pretence. Part of me just wants to frogmarch him around every place that we have ever been until he has what he is looking for.

Over dinner I notice that his expression is more intense. He obviously wants to move this all on as well and I think that he must have been patiently waiting for some time. Now he is closer to getting

what he wants he is probably now even more impatient. His phone rings and he frowns and then answers it. Mouthing sorry to me and raising his eyes up he says, "Hi Bradley. Sorry can't chat I'm out with Bella." He is silent for a while as he listens to his friend and then says, "Ok, we'll stop by on our way home." I look at him quizzically and grinning ruefully he says, "Sorry, I have to drop something off for Bradley that he needs, work related. It is on our way back so I hope that you don't mind the slight detour." I feel unnerved by the thought of seeing Bradley and Tina but know that I can't refuse.

On the way he says, "Sorry baby, I just have to stop by home to get what he wants. It won't take long." As he turns into a gated residence I look at him in surprise. He grins happily and says, "I've moved. I bought this to be closer to work. Come in and have a look around. I haven't been here long so it's still a mess, but I would love to hear your opinion on it." He stops in front of a grand block of Apartments. It looks to be a converted manor house and is very impressive. He lets us in and then stops at a lift in the hallway. "I'm on the top floor so we had better take the lift; otherwise the stairs wear you out." Once we step out of the lift he leads me down an impressive corridor and then opens the door to his flat. I gasp in amazement as I take in the gorgeous surroundings. The flat is huge. It has a very large window that dominates the room which in itself is huge. The decoration is neutral but tasteful and there is a cosy seating area set around a huge fireplace. The room is open plan and I can see an impressive modern kitchen dominating the far end of the room. As he turns on the lights I can see that each area is lit differently which gives the room its own zones.

Obviously enjoying my reaction he smiles and says, "Let me give you the guided tour." He then proceeds to show me every room. There are two immense bedrooms with huge beds in and masses of storage. Both have fabulous en suites with modern fittings. There is also another bathroom and a study. I am very impressed and say, "This is very different from your old flat." He says gently, "I hope that you like it Bella. It is the sort of place that I would have liked to live with you. You deserve the best and I am going to do my utmost to make you fall in love with me again so that I can give you everything that you have ever wanted." I look at him in amazement, the trouble is all I want I already had with Ben. None of this means anything to me, despite what he may think. I am sure that the idea had been to stop here tonight, to impress me and move things on. Inside me I realise that Nathan didn't really know me at all if he thinks that an expensive car and flat would make me go back to him. Looking at him I say, "Shouldn't we be going. Bradley is probably waiting?" He looks disappointed and says, "Yes, you're right. Wait there a minute and I'll grab the file."

As he leaves the room I look around me. There is not much to see that would provide any clues to his dealings, but then I am not surprised. I am sure that any evidence he has is digital and will be stored on his computer somewhere. I wonder how long it will take him to find what he needs. I really hope that it is soon. The longer it takes the harder it will be to keep him at arms length without raising his suspicions. I recognise that it is a fine line that I will have to tread. I think about Melissa. I don't know how she does what she does. I could never pretend to love somebody and sleep with them as she does as a job.

Nathan returns interrupting my thoughts. He smiles and taking my arm again we head back to the car.

On the journey I say, "Couldn't Bradley wait for the file until tomorrow?" Nathan smiles ruefully and says, "No, he is on a course so won't be in all week. This is something he has been working on and they need it sorting by the morning."

"Oh, I see." I say, not really believing anything he has to say.

It takes us about 40 minutes to get to their house. Once again I am surprised by how amazing their house is. It is a new build and has its own driveway and separate garages. An electric gate allows us through and then closes behind us. There is outside lighting that lights up various features of the house and we exit the car and wait by a huge wooden front door, flanked by large pots containing huge bay trees. Almost straight away the door opens and Bradley and

Tina greet us with huge smiles on their faces. Tina rushes forward and envelops me in a hug. "Bella, it's good to see you. We've missed you so much." She drags me inside and the guys follow behind laughing and joking. The hallway is huge and welcoming and I am blown away by how gorgeous their house is. Tina turns to me her eyes sparkling and says, "Let me give you the guided tour whilst Bradley gets us all drinks." Dragging me behind her she shows me around the huge house. It is arranged on three floors and I lose count of how many bedrooms and bathrooms there are. There is a cinema room and a games room on the top floor, with a well stocked bar tucked away in the corner. She indicates outside and says, "Bradley has a gym above the garage with another shower room." I look around me in amazement and say, "I can't take it all in. This house is amazing. You must love it here." Tina smiles happily and I can tell that this is her pride and joy. As we head back downstairs she says in a low voice. "Nathan told me what happened. I am so sorry to hear what a nasty piece of work Ben turned out to be." I stiffen immediately at the sound of his name and noticing it she takes it to mean that I am angry at him. Rubbing my arm she smiles at me and says, "Let's not think about him anymore. Nathan is super excited to have you back in his life and so are we." Looking at her with a puzzled expression I say, "Nathan and I are just friends, nothing more." Grinning at me she says, "Yet." She then giggles and raises her eyes and I can see that she believes that it is only a matter of time before we get back together. I don't enlighten her as it suits me for her to think that way.

As we walk into the large welcoming kitchen I see that Nathan and Bradley are already on the beers. Tina pulls out a bottle of wine and says, "Come on Bella. Let's leave the boys to talk about work and we can have a good old catch up." Grabbing some glasses she pulls me into the living room where a large fireplace houses a roaring fire. We sink down into a comfy settee and she pours me a large glass of wine.

"I'm so glad that you're here Bella. I have missed our chats," Tina says as she hands the wine to me. "You know Nathan has been a nightmare to be around these last few months." Looking at me she raises her eyes and carries on. "He was such an idiot over Melissa and regretted it as soon as she confronted you both on New Years Eve. He thought that he could win you back but when you started seeing Ben Hardcastle he realised that it wasn't going to be that easy."

Although Tina is carrying off from where we left off I don't feel the same about her as I once did. When Nathan and I split up Tina and I met in town for a coffee and she couldn't leave fast enough when she realised that I wasn't going back to Nathan and I haven't heard a word from her ever since. I decide to play along with her to see if I can get any information out of her. She may be involved in the fraud so I need to tread carefully. "A lot has happened since New Year." I say ruefully. She looks at me carefully and says, "Do you think that you and Nathan could ever get back together, or is he fighting a losing battle?" I shrug my shoulders and say, "It is too early to think about getting back together. I enjoy his company though and obviously I loved him not so long ago, but a lot has happened in the last few months and it will take me some time to adjust to it all." I notice that her expression hardens. Apparently that was not what she wanted to hear. Then it changes again as Nathan and Bradley come into the room. She smiles sweetly at them and pats the seat next to her for Bradley to sit down. Nathan sits opposite me and grins at us all. "This is just like old times isn't it?" He says laughing. Bradley also laughs and Tina smiles indulgently at him.

There is something about Tina that unnerves me. I never noticed it before when we were friends but now I am sure that she is hiding her true feelings. Nathan and Bradley continue to joke around and when Nathan goes to pour himself a glass of wine I say, "Nathan, I think that we should be going. You have already had one drink and you need to drive me home." He looks taken aback and there is an awkward silence. Tina recovers first and says to Nathan sternly, "Bella's right. You have had enough if you are driving." Turning to me she says excitedly, "I know, why don't you both stay tonight? We certainly have enough rooms and I can lend you anything you need Bella. We could all have a few drinks and catch up properly." I am taken aback and feel well and truly put on the spot. The last thing I want is to spend the night here and I look at Nathan's excited face with dismay. Noticing my expression he looks down and says, "Another time

Tina. We have work tomorrow and Bella needs to get back." Not to be put off Tina says, "Ok, but what about Saturday night? You could both come for dinner and then stay over." Seeing my face she adds, "Separate rooms of course. Then we could all drink and really chill out." Not wanting to appear rude I say, "My mother has asked if you can come to lunch on Sunday Nathan. Wouldn't that interfere with your plan Tina?" Shaking her head she says, "Of course not. You could then both go to Bella's parents from here." Nathan looks at me, his eyes boring into mine. I can see that he wants me to agree so I shake my head and say, "Well if it's not too much trouble?" Tina claps her hands together in glee and Bradley smiles saying, "Good. That's settled then. It will be just like old times."

I try to ignore the sinking feeling and smile at them both. Nathan jumps up and taking my hand pulls me up. "Come on Bella. I'll take you home."

As we leave I notice a look pass between them all. Something tells me that this has been planned all along.

Chapter 23

The next morning I have to endure the fallout of my date with Nathan from Phoebe. Once I have told her everything that happened she looks at me with a disapproving look. "What?" I say, although in her position I too would think it was all wrong. "You are taking things way too fast with Nathan. You are in no position to start seeing him, as friends or otherwise. It will only end in disaster. He is probably thinking that you are his girlfriend again already, and what about Ben? You can't have switched off your feelings for him over night. Give yourself some space from them both for all your sakes."

I push the pain away at the mention of Ben. I can't think about him. If I did I wouldn't have the strength to see this through. I have to focus on Nathan and the codes. I can't meet her eyes and look down. "I know Phoebs. I don't know what is going on in my head at the moment. All I know is that I owe it to Nathan to hear him out. After all he is as much a victim in all of this as I am." As I say the words I almost choke on them. He is certainly not a victim and if he is planning what I have been led to believe then there will be many more victims from his actions. I hate lying to Phoebe. She doesn't deserve it and the thought that she is angry with me upsets me.

Changing the subject she says, "What are you going to

do about work? You are bound to run into Ben at some point." Looking down I shrug my shoulders. "I may have to look for another job. In fact I suppose I should start looking whilst I'm off."

She looks at me with a horrified expression. "But you love that job. You can't lose everything all at the same time." Collapsing back onto the settee I hold my head in my hands. "It's all a mess isn't it?" I say, holding back the tears as I speak. She rushes over and hugs me. "Don't worry, something will come up. It will all work out in the end."

I decide to go out for a walk. Phoebe has to go to work and I don't fancy just sitting around in the flat. It is a nice day and I head off to the town. As I wander through the streets looking at the tempting shop windows I try to make sense of everything that has happened. If I'm honest I don't really know what I am expected to do. I know that I have to allow Nathan access to the places that we used to go. If he has planted any of the codes on me then he needs to gain access to them. The only reason I agreed to lunch at my parents was in case there were any there. The trouble is how will I know when he has them? He is not exactly going to jump up and down waving them. I feel worn out with the whole situation. Coming across a coffee shop I decide to stop and have a coffee. It is fairly busy so I sit at the back in the corner whilst I once again consider my situation.

I wonder what will happen when he does get them all. Will he still want me or is it all just an act? Then a terrible thought comes into my mind. What if Ben doesn't want me either? He may be unable to forgive me and not want anything to do with me. My stomach is in knots at the thought. I stare morosely into my coffee cup and try to stem the ever present tears from falling. Suddenly my phone rings. Looking at the display I notice that it is Tina. Sighing I answer saying, "Hi Tina, what a nice surprise." She giggles and says, "I'm over here Bella." Looking up with surprise I see her sitting across the coffee shop at another table. She heads over towards me laughing. "You should have seen your face Bella. You were far away and didn't notice me when you came in. I thought it would be funny to ring you and surprise you." I laugh and try to look happy to see her. "What are you doing here Tina, are you shopping?" She nods. "Yes, I am indulging in some retail therapy today. Would you like to join me?" I try to look pleased and say, "Yes, that would be great." We grab our bags and head off towards the nearest shop. Tina excitedly drags me around several stores and doesn't hold back. She spends a small fortune and puts it all on her credit card. Money appears to be no object and I wonder how often she does this. I help her carry her bags and she says, "Let me treat you to lunch. It's the least I can do after all of your help with my shopping." She laughs and I look at her thinking how false she has become. She drags me into an Italian restaurant that doesn't look cheap and sinks down into her seat. The bags are all around us and I feel embarrassed at the amount of purchases that she has made. We order our lunch and she looks at me intently. "You know what Bella, if you got back with Nathan, you wouldn't ever have to work again." I look at her in amazement and she laughs. "Bradley and Nathan are earning a fortune. It doesn't matter what I spend, he earns it back right away. You wouldn't need to ever see Ben again and Nathan would look after you well. It's every woman's dream and the fact that he is so gorgeous makes it a win win situation." I feel the disgust rising up within me. She is so shallow. If she thinks that I am impressed by her words then she has another thing coming. I would hate to just sit around all day, pampering myself and shopping on someone else's money. Even if they did earn it legitimately. The fact that their money is probably anything but makes it worse. I want to stand up and slap her and then tell her what I really think of her. Instead I try to feign interest and say, "It certainly looks attractive. I mean who wouldn't want a life of luxury with no worries. You are very lucky."

My words seem hollow to me but she appears pleased and leans forward, excitement shining in her eyes. "You only have to say the word Bella. Nathan would be back with you like a shot. He wants nothing more and we could all have such a fabulous life together." I nod as words are failing me at the moment. I just want to get away from her but decide that I should use the time wisely and try to find out a bit more about the situation. "So Tina, when did you give up your job?" She has the grace to blush and says, "Oh about four months ago. Bradley said he would prefer it if I took it easy and looked after the home instead. It also means I have more time and energy to devote to him, if you know what I mean." She giggles and raises her eyes suggestively. I feel sick. Since when did she aspire to become a Stepford wife? I don't think that I could hate her anymore than I do at this moment. Instead I smile as though I am impressed and she carries on. "I mean, I did join a gym to keep in trim. I have a personal trainer who is fit in every sense of the word." She giggles again and carries on. "Then there is my weekly hair appointment just before I get my nails done. I meet up with friends and we organise days out and get togethers at each others homes. I spend a lot of time shopping and am generally extremely busy." Trying to look impressed I say, "It all sounds like fun. You are so lucky. When are you getting married? I remember that you were engaged the last time I saw you when I finished with Nathan. Have you set a date yet?"

Grinning excitedly she says, "Bradley said that they are working on a really big job at the moment and as soon as it is finished we will go abroad and get married. He has said that I can choose anywhere in the world, money will be no object." Painting a smile on my face I think about what she has said. She is either stupid or hasn't got a clue what is really going on. How on earth does she think that an IT employee of an Insurance company could earn the sort of money that she is talking about? Testing this out I say, "The Insurance Company must pay extremely large bonuses in that case." Her expression changes and she looks around her furtively. Lowering her voice she leans in towards me and says, "Between me and you, the Insurance Company is just the day job. They are working on a joint project on the side. It is very hush hush but when they have finished they have told me that we will be set up for life." I look interested, hoping that she will tell me more but then she leans back and her face settles back to her normal expression and she laughs saying, "This is so nice isn't it? I hope that you do end up back together. It will be fun to be the fearsome foursome again." I don't say anything but study her for a moment. I then look at my watch and feign surprise. "Oh no, is that the time? I'm sorry Tina but I have to go. I promised Phoebe that I would be there when she gets back from work. Here let me give you the money for my meal. I had a great time and I am sorry to have to rush off." She waves the money away and says, "No Bella, I insist, my treat. Don't worry I had fun. I look forward to seeing you on Saturday. I'll call a cab and the driver can help me with my bags. The large tip usually helps." Once again she laughs shrilly and I can't get out of there quickly enough.

Chapter 24

I can't get home fast enough. I don't remember Tina being so shallow, but then again I am obviously a terrible judge of character, given the revelations about Nathan.

I am pleased to see that Phoebe is home. I need some sort of normality back in my life after the last few days. However it soon becomes apparent that she is not herself. She looks at me awkwardly and I wonder what the matter is? "Phoebs are you ok?" I say, looking at her with concern. She sighs and says, "I'm sorry Bella. I am worried about you that's all. Something doesn't add up and I can't work out what it is." Looking down I blush. I feel terrible. I long to confide in her but I am sworn to secrecy. I can feel her watching me so I try to look as normal as I can and say, "I know it's been a stressful few days. I am trying to get my head around it all myself. It feels strange not working and with Nathan hanging around I can't seem to sort my head out." She races over to me and grabs my hands. "Keep away from him for a while Bella. Please, for me. I don't know why but there is something bothering me and I think that you should use this time to gather your thoughts without any distractions from any of the men in your life." I nod and shrug my shoulders. "I know you're right Phoebs but I feel as though I owe Nathan something. He has put a lot of effort into bringing out the truth and I sort of feel indebted to him." Her eyes narrow but she says nothing. I can feel myself blushing under her scrutiny and then she releases my hands and says, "Anyway, let's just have a nice evening in together. Boris is working late so it will be just like old times." I feel myself relax and just look forward to a night of uncomplicated TV and chat with my best friend.

Saturday soon comes and I feel anxious as to how I am going to broach the subject of my sleepover at Tina and Bradley's with Phoebe. Luckily I am worrying unnecessarily as Phoebe informs me that her and Boris are going to stay with some friends this weekend. "Will you be ok B?" she says, looking at me anxiously. Nodding I say, "Yes, of course. Go and enjoy yourselves. Don't worry about me." I heave an inward sigh of relief. This is replaced by a nervous feeling at the thought of the coming weekend. I know that Nathan will want to be more than just friends and it is going to be difficult to juggle the situation. Once they leave I set about packing for the night ahead. I really want to take my canvas picture but realise how ridiculous it would look and may draw attention to it. I pack an overnight bag and get ready. At 6.30pm on the dot the doorbell rings and on opening the door I find Nathan lounging in the doorway. "Hi baby." He says, looking at me with his cheeky grin. "You're looking good as always."

Smiling at him I say, "Hi Nathan. I'm ready if you are?" He looks taken aback and I wonder if he had wanted to come in. Maybe he needs to look for something in the flat so I say, "Oh, actually, you had better come in for a minute. I think I've forgotten something." He looks relieved and I usher him in. "I won't be long, sorry." I shout as I go back into my room. I decide to give him 5 minutes which should be long enough for him to find whatever it is that he may be looking for.

Sitting on the bed I look at my picture. Tears spring into my eyes again and I bite my lip to stop them. Suddenly on hearing the door open I look up in surprise to see Nathan entering the room. Jumping up from the bed in confusion I say, "Sorry Nathan, I'm ready now if you are?"

He moves purposefully towards me and my heart sinks as I see the look on his face. I am annoyed with myself. I should have left when he first arrived and now I have put myself in a compromising position. Approaching me his eyes hold mine, his gaze is soft and gentle and I feel a lump forming in my throat. Sitting down on the bed he pats it saying, "Bella, sit next to me for a minute. I want to talk to you first before we leave." Swallowing hard I sit on the edge as far away from him as I can. Reaching out he tucks my hair behind my ear. "I just wanted to say that I am glad that you agreed to this weekend. It means a lot to me and even though I know that we aren't together, I hope that you will learn to love me again." My eyes feel as huge as saucers and I don't know what to say. He picks up my hand and squeezes it. "I love you Bella. We were happy once and can be again, if you just give us a chance."

Moving my hand away I look down. In a soft voice I say, "I need time Nathan. A lot has changed in the last few months and I don't know where I am emotionally. You will need to give me time to work out what I want." I hear him draw in a sharp breath and I look up at him, seeing the disappointment in his eyes. Quickly I stand up. "Come on, let's go. Bradley and Tina will be waiting for us."

As I exit the room I notice that Nathan doesn't immediately follow me. I leave him and busy myself making sure that everything is turned off. I wonder if he is looking at anything and wish that I could see what he is doing. Seeing the door open I watch as he comes out looking dejected. He smiles ruefully at me saying, "Sorry Bella. I just needed a moment to get my thoughts together. It's just that I have waited so long to even be friends again. I am afraid that I am impatient for more. It's ok though, I understand and we will take things as slowly as you need to."

Relieved I reply, "Thanks Nathan. I am sure that things will work out in the end. It's just that everything has happened so quickly." He spies my bag on the floor and picking it up changes his voice back to the carefree, fun Nathan that I fell in love with and says, "Come on then. Let's go and have some fun."

Chapter 25

It feels strange being at Bradley and Tina's house with Nathan. We always used to meet up before and enjoyed many a similar evening. I feel awkward around them now and am on edge, hoping that I don't give anything away and am constantly looking at them for anything out of the ordinary. Nathan is being his usual self and keeps the conversation light and has us all in stitches. This is him at his best and it reminds me of happier times, when we were in love and totally happy with each other. Part of me regrets what I have

lost. Ben is so different and is much more intense and serious. He has more of a mysterious character and isn't as light hearted as Nathan in company. Thinking of Ben sends shivers through me. I miss him so much. Even the thought of him makes me want him and I quickly push away the thought that I may never see him again.

I notice that they are all drinking far too much as usual which I am actually quite pleased about. Nathan isn't so good when he has a drink and normally goes out for the count. Even though I have my own room tonight, I wouldn't put it past him to try anything on with me. After dinner we take another bottle of wine into the living room and congregate around the fire. Tina is sitting with her feet up on Bradley and Nathan is sitting next to me on the settee opposite them. He has his arm running along the back of the settee, almost touching me but not quite. Tina suddenly starts laughing and says, "Wouldn't it be great if you two got back together again before Christmas? We could all go skiing afterwards." Bradley laughs nodding in agreement and Nathan brings his arm down so that it is resting on my shoulders. He pulls me towards him saying, "One step at a time Tina. The fact that Bella is here at all is major progress."

Smiling thinly I can't help but notice that his arm stays where it is. I want to move away but don't want to embarrass Nathan in front of his friends. Tina carries on. "Do you know I love Christmas? I spend ages planning it, months even. I have even started writing my Christmas cards, and it's only October." Bradley laughs and raises his eyes up. "That's Tina for you. If she hasn't got a list book on the go then she gets palpitations, isn't that right my darling." She grins at him and then kisses him softly. Nathan laughs and says, "Bella's the same. I mean do you remember your Christmas notebook Bella?" Pulling a face at him I say, "What's wrong with my Christmas notebook?" I can see that Bradley and Tina are now looking interested and he teases me by saying, "Well Bella has this notebook that she has had since way back. In it she has lists and lists of Christmas planning. Menus, present ideas, in fact anything connected to Christmas at all." Tina laughs and says, "I need one of them. I love a good planning notebook." Nathan grins and says, "She has listed every one in there that she sends cards to. It stays the same every year and she never changes it. She just adds to it if there is somebody new to send a card to." Rather sharply I say, "What's wrong with that? I am sure that there are loads of people like me. It saves me writing it out every year. We're not all like you and keep everything on our hard drive. I mean what if my computer failed, where would I be then?"

He laughs and squeezes my shoulder. "Do you still have it?" says Tina and I notice that the atmosphere has changed slightly. It seems as though they are waiting for my answer as if it is important. Then I realise that maybe this is what Nathan has been looking for. I feel confused though. Why would anything be in there? I mean it only comes out once a year and is hidden away for the rest of it. To my knowledge he has never even looked in it, let alone stashed anything in it. Trying to look relaxed and oblivious to their interest I decide to test it out. Shrugging my shoulders I say, "Actually, I'm not sure if I do." I feel Nathan tense beside me and because I am looking so closely I see Bradley's eyes narrow and Tina's lips tighten. Ordinarily I wouldn't notice their reactions but as I am looking specifically for them I notice them very much. Bingo, my Christmas notebook is the key to whatever they are planning. Nathan laughs in disbelief and says, "What do you mean, you're not sure if you do? You have had that book for years; you can't have got rid of it." I risk looking at him with what I hope is an innocent expression. "I can't remember where I put it. I mean after all, I had rather a lot to deal with after last Christmas and my usual routine went out of the window." I see a look pass between them all and Tina laughs nervously saying, "Oh I'm sure you'll find it. You probably put it in with the Christmas decorations or something. If I were you I would start looking now. Despite the fact that its October Christmas isn't that far away you know." She laughs again and we all join in. They have told me what I needed to know though, even though they don't realise it. I know exactly where it is, in fact where it always is, in my bedroom at my parent's house, in a box on the top shelf of my wardrobe, with the rest of my Christmas cards and decorations. They continue chatting away and after a while Tina says, "Who's for coffee?" "I'll help you," I say jumping up; glad to get away from the invasion of Nathan's arm. As we head towards the kitchen I say, "That was a lovely meal Tina. You really are very kind to go to so much trouble." She smiles saying, "It's my pleasure Bella. We don't actually have that many friends and it's nice to be able to relax with some for a change. I mean Bradley works all the time and my new friends don't really know the real me. It's nice not to have to keep up the pretence of being something

I'm not."

I look at her in surprise. "What do you mean Tina? Surely you can just be yourself. You are the same person that I know, just because you suddenly have more money it doesn't change you inside." Leaning against the worktop she frowns. "The trouble is Bella;

Bradley's new friends are all very wealthy and live a different life to you and I. I am always feeling the need to keep up with them and do the things that they do. I'm not stupid though and know that they look down on me."

"Then get new friends," I say tartly. She blushes and says, "I lost touch with all of my old friends. A lot of them were jealous and uninterested in the things that I do now. They can't relate to me anymore and I hate to admit it but I am lonely." She bites her lip and tears well up in her eyes.

Looking at her I am in total shock. I never expected this. I thought that she was relishing her new life. As I look at her with surprise, for some reason I don't feel any sympathy for her. Before I can say anything Nathan bursts into the room and Tina turns away to gather up the drinks tray. "Where are you, you're taking ages with those drinks?" He suddenly grabs hold of me and in one sweep lifts me over his shoulder. Laughing he says, "You are coming with me. I don't want to spend my evening talking to Bradley when you are around."

Tina laughs at us as Nathan carries me from the room. I struggle to get out of his grip but he holds on and only lets me down when we reach the sitting room. Depositing me onto the settee he lands beside me and grins triumphantly. Tina brings up the rear with the drinks. In some ways I am glad of the distraction from Tina's problems. I didn't know what to say and wonder why she felt the need to say something to me in the first place. Grinning sheepishly at me she hands me a coffee and I raise my eyes up as if to check that she is ok. She gives me a small smile and a slight nod and then sits back down next to Bradley.

I try to steer the conversation towards their new job at the Insurance Company. I am intrigued to know what they do there but Nathan says, "We don't want to talk about work tonight Bella. It's all really boring and you would be asleep before long. I would much rather talk about all of us and the possibility that we may book a pre Christmas weekend away together." I look at him in shock. What on earth is he thinking? Why would I go away with them?

Tina claps her hands together with excitement and looks at me, her eyes shining. "Oh please say you'll come Bella. We can go as friends, nothing else. It would be so much fun." Bradley laughs saying, "Yes, let's do it. You can choose if you want, just let us know when and where."

I can see Nathan looking at me hopefully and I shrug my shoulders. "I'm not sure. I will be going back to work after next weekend and will be really busy once again with the pre Christmas rush. I don't think I will have the time." Nathan looks at me with determination and says, "Then next weekend it will be. We can tie it up with your birthday Bella and celebrate it properly for once. No strings attached just as friends." They are all looking at me with such hope that I can only nod and say, "Ok, but just as friends, nothing more."

Nathan puts his arm around me and squeezes me with delight. "Thanks Bella, I will make sure that you have a birthday to remember." Tina and Bradley look at me happily and I can only wonder what the real reason behind this trip really is.

Soon the evening tails off and everyone is yawning. Tina says, "Come on Bella; let me show you to your room. You must be exhausted." Gratefully I follow her upstairs. She shows me to a lovely guest bedroom that is very tastefully decorated in creams and beige. It has its on en suite which I am glad of. I feel the need to be alone as it has been quite an ordeal for me and wish that I had never agreed to stay. Before she leaves me Tina suddenly gives me an unexpected hug. "Thanks Bella. I know this has been difficult for you. I am sure that it will all get easier as time goes on. I am convinced that you will soon realise that you and Nathan are meant to be together. It's still early days though, but you are doing really well." I smile weakly at her and then thankfully she leaves me alone. As I get ready I feel more and more convinced that she is wrong. There is only one man for me and that's Ben. The day that all of this is over can't come quickly enough for me.

Chapter 26

I sleep quite fitfully; I can't relax as I keep on expecting Nathan to knock on the door. I wouldn't have put it past him, but thankfully he keeps his distance. We are due to go to my parent's house for lunch and I wonder if he will use the opportunity to look for the Christmas notebook.
Once I am ready I venture downstairs. As I leave my room I see Nathan coming out of a neighbouring bedroom. Seeing me he smiles. "Morning baby, did you sleep well?" "Yes thanks Nathan, did you?" I say returning his smile. He comes over and pulls me towards him. He leans down towards me and his eyes look softly at me. "Bella, this is torture for me. Knowing that you were in the next room to me all night was difficult. I wanted to be with you so badly and I will do anything for us to get back what we once had." Pulling back sharply I see a hurt expression flash across his face. Looking down I say, "I'm sorry Nathan. I didn't mean to upset you. It is difficult for me too. Just give me time, a lot has happened and I need to adjust to things." His face relaxes again and he says, "Of course. We will take it one step at a time. Right then, friends it is." Grabbing my hand he pulls me off downstairs.

Tina has made a fabulous breakfast and won't accept any help from me. "Sit down Bella. You are guest and I want you to relax. Bradley can help out if necessary." Bradley grimaces and Nathan laughs. Trying to relax I join in with their general chit chat and before long it is time to leave to go to my parent's house. As we say our goodbyes I notice the eager look that Tina gives me as she says, "Don't forget next weekend Bella. We can have a really good catch up then. Maybe we can even ditch the guys and find some alone time. Oh and I wouldn't mind if you find your Christmas notebook letting me have a look at it. I could do with sorting one out for myself and now is the perfect time to set one up."

Nathan interrupts and says, "We could look for it at your parent's house if you want Bella. There's no time like the present." They all look at me expectantly so I shrug and laugh saying, "If you like, although you may be disappointed when you see it Tina. I mean it's nothing special, that is if I can find it." I can't resist adding, looking with satisfaction at how their smiles just slip slightly at my words.

As Nathan grabs our bags I thank them both and soon we are waving at them as we drive away. I feel relief at the thought that I have survived the ordeal, just lunch to go and then I can't wait to get home.

As we pull into my parent's drive I can see my mum at the door. My heart sinks. She will be ecstatic that Nathan is here. Suddenly I feel extremely guilty. It is not fair to raise their hopes like this. They will want me to get back with him and I know that it is going to break their hearts when they find out the real reason for my split with Ben. Nathan looks at me and grins. "I have missed your parents, I feel as though I am

coming home." I smile but say nothing, knowing that the next few hours are going to be very trying.
As soon as we get out of the car my mum races over and hugs Nathan tightly. "Nathan darling, we have missed you so much. How are you?" Pulling back to look at him she frowns and says, "You look thinner. Are you eating properly? Never mind come in and I will feed you up." Nathan grins as I snort, "Don't mind me will you?" My mum laughs and hugs me too. "Sorry honey. I'm just so pleased to see Nathan that's all. It's just like old times isn't it?" Nathan laughs and puts his arm around her. "I've missed you too, and your cooking. As you can see I am wasting away without it."
She drags him inside and I follow them in dreading the next few hours. The thought of them fawning over Nathan is making me angry already. My dad comes to greet us when we are inside. "Great to see you son." He says obviously quite choked and I wince at his choice of words. Nathan grins at him and follows him inside. Mum turns to me and I notice the excited gleam in her eye. "Bella, it's so good to see you two together. I can't thank Nathan enough for saving you from that monster Ben. I hope that you will soon feel able to sort out any differences you have and get back together." Raising my eyes up I say, "Don't get your

hopes up mum. I have just agreed to spend some time with him as friends, that's all. We are certainly a long way from getting back together; I just want to make that perfectly clear. Please don't go on about it anymore. I know that you prefer Nathan over Ben that much is obvious, however you don't know him like I do and I can't just switch off my feelings because of what Nathan has found out."

Mum looks at me with concern. "I'm sorry darling. I know that all of this has been hard on you. Don't worry, we'll go easy today. The trouble is we are so happy to see him and never thought that you should have split up in the first place." Smiling I say, "Come on, let's go inside." Linking arms with my mother we head off to find the others.

I feel much more comfortable being at home. It was very stressful being at Bradley and Tina's and I couldn't relax. At least here I can leave everyone else to talk without appearing rude.

I help my mum prepare the lunch and enjoy the feeling of familiarity in my surroundings. My dad is watching the football with Nathan and it is very much like old times. I feel a pang as I watch them. They have never accepted Ben like they do Nathan. They have always felt a little uncomfortable with him and I never felt that I could leave him with them for long. Nathan has spent many hours with my dad, going to football matches and down the pub. It used to make me laugh to see how well they got on and I loved the fact that they were so close. Now I hate it. Turning my attention away from them I say to my mum, "How's

Amy? I haven't seen her in ages." Amy is my sister and is currently living in Ireland due to her husband Simon's job. Mum smiles. "She is fine. She called last night and is planning to come home for Christmas. Between me and you I think that she may have something to tell us." Raising my eyes up I say, "Are you sure you're not just hoping that she has some news?" My mum is desperate to become a Grandmother and is forever hinting to Amy that the clock is ticking. Amy is too busy leading a fantastic life over there to worry about starting a family just yet. Her and her husband have very high powered jobs and a great social life. They are enjoying life to the full and I would have thought that starting a family was furthermost from their minds.

"Go and see if the men need another drink will you?" mum says interrupting my thoughts. I wander into the living room and laugh at their excited faces watching the match. Nathan pats the seat next to him and says, "Sit here Bella. This game is great. We are 2-0 already and it's not even half time yet." Pulling a face I say, "Absolutely not. You know that I hate football. I just wondered if you both needed more drinks."

Nathan smiles and asks for a beer as does my dad. Looking at them both so happy a part of me wishes that things had been different. If Ben hadn't come along, Nathan and I would be married now and life would be easy. Then I am pulled back to reality. Of course it wouldn't be, happy ever after. Nathan is planning some sort of criminal master plan and we may already be in prison if he had gone ahead with it.

I would have been dragged in as an accomplice and our cosy new life would have been anything but. With a sudden thought I wonder if Nathan ever really wanted to marry me. It may have all been a set up to get me onside and use me as a cover. As I think back over our time together certain things come into my head and a terrible feeling comes over me. It all went so quickly from when I first met him to his proposal. Ben's words come back to me, "Seven months is not long enough to know somebody before committing the rest of your life to them." I remember that Nathan was bored with the wedding planning and said, "Just you tell me when and where and I will be there. Just tell me what to do and I will do it. I want it to be perfect for you so whatever you want just do it." At the time I felt put out and now thinking about it I remember how annoyed I was. I even let Phoebe plan my wedding. It turned out ok in the end as when I called it off she married Boris instead.

I set about getting the drinks, these thoughts buzzing around my mind. As I hand the drinks over Nathan's fingers brush against mine. He looks at me and his eyes soften. I remember how he used to make me feel. We couldn't get enough of each other and I don't want to think that it was all an act. He must have loved me, he couldn't have pretended for that amount of time surely? Then I think of Ben and how he makes me feel. It is nothing like how Nathan did. I have never felt such intense reactions to anybody. When I am not with him something is missing. When we are together I feel safe and at home where I belong. Even now I feel incomplete. I suddenly feel a sharp pain within me. I miss him so much. It has only been a week yet it feels like a year. I can't help it and tears spring into my eyes. Nathan looks at me with concern and I can tell that he thinks it is down to him. He looks happily at me and whispers softly, "Come and sit with me baby. We'll get through this, I love you. I will take care of you, you're safe with me." I smile but pull away. "I must help my mum. Anyway, I can't interrupt the game can I?" He laughs and I can see that he thinks that things will get back to normal soon.

As I help my mum she turns the conversation to Ben. "Have you heard from Ben at all?" she says quietly, looking at me with concern. My eyes fill up and I shake my head. "No, nothing. My things were returned so I didn't have to see him." She looks at me with a grim expression. "Coward. Probably can't face you after what Nathan found out. And to think that you nearly lost Nathan over him. Thank goodness he loves you as much as he does otherwise you would never have known." Feeling angry I snap back. "Just leave it mum. I don't want to hear another word about Ben." Her mouth tightens and then I realise that Nathan has entered the kitchen and heard every word. Coming over he puts his arm around me and pulls me towards him. "It's ok Bella. He's gone now. We won't mention him again. Let's just concentrate on us now and put the last year behind us." My mum looks at us happily and I feel as though I am in a nightmare. "Call your dad Bella, dinner's ready. Let's just enjoy the rest of our day."

Chapter 27

Lunch is fabulous as usual. Nathan and my parents talk constantly which gives me time to gather my thoughts. I don't feel like joining in and just give appropriate answers when necessary. Any spark in me died when I walked away from Ben and they are annoying me the way they are all carrying on as before. Once lunch is over my mum says, "Leave the dishes Bella, I will do them later. You and Nathan go and relax and I will bring you in a cup of tea."
This is the last thing that I want to do so I say, "No mum, let me help you tidy up, it's the least I can do." She won't have it though and is quite stern. "Absolutely not. I won't hear another word." Nathan laughs and then says, "I know Bella, why don't I help you look for that notebook that Tina wants to see. It may be here." I freeze inside at his words and my

mum says, "What notebook is that Bella?" Trying to dismiss it I say, "Oh just that Christmas one that I write my lists in." She looks amazed, "That old thing. Why on earth does Tina want to see that?" Laughing Nathan says, "She thinks it sounds like a good idea. She is into her lists and wanted a few pointers in setting up her own." Mum looks at us thoughtfully and says, "I'm sure it must be in your wardrobe Bella. Go and see whilst I make the drinks." Suddenly I don't know what to do. Should I let him have it or am I meant to locate it and then keep it from him and await further instructions? I feel confused as Nathan pulls me along with him towards the stairs. "Come on, we can find it and then you can show Tina next weekend." Nodding I follow him and soon we are in my old room.

Sitting on the bed Nathan watches me as I open the wardrobe. "Do you want me to lift anything out?" he says, looking at me intently. He says it quite casually but I can feel the tension. Even though he appears laid back and uninterested, I can sense that he is on edge. He is smiling but his eyes have hardened and I can see a muscle working in his face as he watches me. Trying to look relaxed I shake my head. "It's ok, I can manage." I can feel his scrutiny as I lift the box down. Inside are all of my decorations and spare cards. I see the notebook and wonder what on earth it contains that is so important to him. With a flourish I pull it out and say, "Here it is, not lost at all." Looking at him I can see the relief in his face. I can tell that he is itching to get his hands on it and I hold onto it with a vice like grip. As I flick through the pages I exclaim, "I can't imagine why Tina needs to see this. Surely she can make her own one up." Nathan gets up and comes over and I watch him as he looks at the book in my hands. "No, it does seem strange," he says distractedly. Reaching out he goes to take it from me and I move away. I see his eyes narrow but he laughs and says, "If you want Bella, I could take it and put the information onto a disc for you?" Laughing I say,

"Absolutely not Nathan. I wouldn't want it on a computer. This notebook has been with me for years and does its job perfectly well. I'll take it and show Tina next weekend as asked, thanks for the offer but no thanks." I can sense his frustration and then luckily we hear my mum calling. "Have you found it? Tea's ready when you are." Grinning at him I say, "Come on, let's go before it gets cold."

Before I can leave though Nathan pulls me towards him. He looks at me gently and says, "Just a minute Bella. I have had a lovely weekend. Being here with you is a dream come true. I never thought that I ever would be again. I know that we are just friends but there is something that I need to do and it can't wait another minute." Before I know what is happening he takes the book from my hand and leans towards me. He holds me firmly to him and then kisses me gently at first and then more urgently. I am stunned. He is holding me so tightly that I cannot move. As he kisses me I realise that I feel nothing. I used to love kissing him and we couldn't keep our hands off each other. Now it just feels wrong. I am glad about that as it would be awful if I still loved him. His kiss becomes more urgent and I feel him harden against me. He pulls me closer and I feel his hand move down my back and reach underneath my top, touching my bare flesh. I hear him groan and he pushes me back towards the bed. Startled I pull away and look at him with a shocked expression. Grinning he says, "I'm sorry baby, you know that I could never resist you."

I hear my mother calling again and still in shock I grab

the notebook and quickly say, "Come on. She will wonder what we are doing." Laughing he throws me a wicked look and says, "I know what I wish we were doing." Seeing the look I give him he throws his hands up in the air saying, "Ok, I know I was out of line. You shouldn't be so sexy baby. You know that I could never get enough of you and it's been torture this weekend being so near you and yet so far." Without answering I just head off downstairs. My mind is buzzing away with everything that has just happened and I am glad to reach the safety of the living room.

"There you are," my mum says and I see her throw a knowing look over to my dad who grins. Nathan also sees the look pass between them and winks at me. Seeing the notebook in my hand my mum says, "Oh you found it then. I thought that it would be there." Nathan says, "I offered to put it all on the computer for Bella so that it would be safe, but she won't let me."

My mum snorts saying, "Quite right too. Who wants to be bothered looking at things on a computer all of the time. Pen and paper is more than adequate." I smile, thanking my mum silently. She hates computers and I am grateful for it as I see the resigned look pass over Nathan's face. I decide to put the book in my bag and will think about what I have to do with it later. I have a week before we all go away so am hoping that I will get further instructions.

After saying goodbye to my parents Nathan drops me home. On the journey he tells me how much he enjoyed the weekend and seeing my parents again.

"Next time you must come to my parents. They have missed you and can't wait to catch up with you again." I smile but think that it would be best not to go there. Things are already getting out of hand and I am not sure how much longer I will be able to keep him at arms length without a scene. We soon reach the flat and he says, "Aren't you going to invite me in Bella? I don't want to leave you." Turning he looks at me and says, "Please baby. Let me back into your life. Let me stay and I will prove to you once and for all that I love you." I blush as he is looking at me so earnestly and I know what he means when he says that he wants to stay. Smiling weakly I say, "Not now Nathan. Phoebe and Boris are back, their car is here and I need to catch up with them." Not giving up he says, "Come home with me then. I don't want you to go. I just want to feel close to you again. Please let me baby, I can make it all go away." Shaking my head I say firmly, "No Nathan. You agreed to take things slowly. I will see you next weekend. I may have changed my mind by then. It is still too early." He smiles ruefully saying, "Well you can't blame me for trying." Grabbing my bag I leave him in the car. I don't look back as I head towards the flat, feeling his eyes burning into my back as I go. I just hope that I can find out what to do before next weekend. The last thing I want is to have to go away with them. Something tells me that I won't be able to hold him off for much longer.

Chapter 28

I spent a lovely evening with Phoebe and Boris. They were surprised when I told them what I had been up to and I noticed how disapproving Phoebe was. She seems quite cross and I don't blame her. In her shoes I would have been the same.

Once I get to my room I sit on my bed and take the notebook out of my bag. I look at my picture on the wall and hope that there is some sort of surveillance camera in it. I need them to know that I have found what Nathan is looking for.

As I look at the picture I try to imagine that Ben is looking at me. I want to be close to him again. This week feels like a year and it is driving me mad. As I flick through the book I notice that nothing appears to have changed and I can't imagine what is in here that Nathan needs so much. My phone rings, startling me out of my task. I can see that it is Nathan and with a sinking feeling I answer it.

"Nathan, hi, did you forget something?" He laughs, "Only you baby, but then you know that already. I just wanted to say thank you for a lovely weekend. I am counting the days until next weekend already." Trying to sound normal I say, "Yes, it was fun. Thank you for arranging it." His voice grows more urgent and he says, "Meet me this week one evening. I don't want to wait another week before seeing you again." Sighing inwardly I try not to sound irritated. "I'm sorry

Nathan. I need a bit of space. Everything has happened so fast. Just let me have some time on my own and I will see you next weekend as arranged."
Sounding disappointed he says, "Ok, I understand. But I warn you, I will make sure that next weekend is so amazing that you won't ever want to let me go." He laughs wickedly and I say, "Just let me know the arrangements. Good night Nathan and have a good week."
"You too baby. I love you, I never stopped, just remember that." He hangs up and I lay back on my bed, glad to be alone at last. At least I have a few days to work up to what I know will be an extremely draining weekend.

The next few days pass by uneventfully and I am getting increasingly anxious about the coming weekend. I have not been sleeping well as everything is whirring away in my mind. I think about phoning Ben at the store but can't risk it. His boss had told me to contact nobody and I am feeling very frustrated. Luckily Phoebe has asked me to meet her for lunch at the gallery and I welcome the distraction. We haven't had much time to talk and it will be nice to get out and spend some time with her. I haven't let the notebook out of my sight since I discovered its importance. I wouldn't put it past Nathan to find some excuse to get into the flat and take it.
As I push open the doors to the gallery I feel a sense of calm come over me. I love where Phoebe works. It

is so quiet and serene. The works of Art are placed in several rooms and I enjoy wandering around taking them all in.

Soon I see Phoebe and she comes over and greets me warmly. "Bella, you made it. I am looking forward to our lunch." I notice that she suddenly looks nervous and won't meet my eyes. This is strange and out of character. She is usually an open book and I wonder what the matter is. "Is everything ok Phoebs? You seem distracted." Smiling she says, "Oh I'm fine, just a little busy at the moment. In fact there is something that I have to do urgently before we can go. Would you mind waiting for me? I shouldn't be more than half an hour and you can wait in the staff room and make yourself a cup of tea."

Raising my eyes up I say, "Don't worry Phoebs I can just look around at the exhibits." To my surprise she looks at me with a sudden determined expression saying, "No, go and have the tea. I am expecting a buyer and his party to look at the Monroe collection. It would be better if you waited behind the scenes, so to speak."

She looks quite guilty and I don't want to add to her obvious stress so just smile saying, "Ok, lead the way."

She looks relieved and I realise that this sale must be an important one. Showing me to the staff room door she says, "Go in Bella. I won't keep you long. Make yourself at home."

She hurries off and I push the door open and head

inside to wait. However as soon as the door closes I am aware that I am not alone. Spinning around I am shocked to see who is behind the door.

"Hello Bella." The blood drains from my face and tears flow down my cheeks. "Ben! What, how, I mean…." The words spill out but make no sense. He is looking at me with such an intense expression and the sight of him standing there is almost too much to bear. In no time at all he covers the distance between us and takes me in his arms and holds me tightly against him. My legs buckle from underneath me and I sob uncontrollably. Stroking my hair he whispers, "It's alright Bella. Let it all out. I'm so sorry, you've been very brave."

I cling on to him, not wanting to let him go. Pulling away I can see the love in his eyes as he takes out a hanky and wipes my eyes. Then holding my head gently in place he kisses me so sweetly. I pull him closer and then the kiss becomes more passionate. He is like a drug that I have been deprived of. I can't get enough of him.

He pushes me against the wall, pinning me against it with his legs and kisses me relentlessly. The need for him is overwhelming and any thoughts of where we are and what has happened are out of my mind. I want him now and I don't want him to stop. Suddenly he checks himself and pulls back. I gasp at his withdrawal and look at him in confusion. Holding a finger to his lips he reaches inside my top, near my neck. He draws out the badger necklace and smiles happily at me. He removes it from around my neck and places it inside a bag that he draws out from his pocket. Still indicating for me to stay silent he goes over and locks the door. I watch him, wondering what this is all about. He goes over to the sink and turns on the taps. There is a TV in the corner which he also turns on and turns the volume up. Then he approaches me again and pulls me close. He whispers in my ear, "Now we can talk." I look at him in confusion and he says in a low voice. "I have been going out of my mind since you left and couldn't wait any longer to see you. We haven't got long and more than anything I want to make love to you right here and now, but we need to talk."

I look at him knowing that my desire for him must be written all over my face, but I recognise that he needs to tell me something important. Before he begins I whisper, "I didn't want to leave you Ben. I know what is going on and I had to do what I did to protect you. I know that you were trying to protect me but I have to finish it."

His features harden and I can feel how tense he is. "I would have found a way Bella. I didn't want you in any more danger. I have been out of my mind with worry and can't bear the thought that you are with him." Kissing him gently I say, "I am not with him in any other sense than to accomplish what needs to be done. It is necessary to be around him but I am keeping my distance. I have found out what it is he needs though and I don't know if I am meant to give it to him or to you." Ben nods saying, "I know. I have been watching and listening so know what stage you

are at."
I look at him in surprise and he laughs quietly. "The picture has a camera in; I knew that you would keep it with you. I watch you when you sleep; it's my way of staying close to you. When you were away this weekend I have been going out of my mind, wondering if you were safe from him." Smiling shyly I say, "I like knowing that you are watching me. I hoped that was the case. Nathan didn't come near me, except…" I feel him stiffen and his expression darkens. Sighing I say, "He did kiss me at my parent's house. I was taken by surprise and luckily my mum interrupted us. I think it was done to distract me from the notebook." He hisses, "I know what happened." Looking at him in confusion I say, "How did you know?" Pointing to the bag in his pocket he says, "The necklace has a microphone in it. I can hear what you say, so I know everything."

I look surprised and his expression softens. "I trust you Bella, the microphone is there to keep you safe and for us to gather evidence against Nathan."

I have to ask and say, "What next Ben? Please tell me that it is over. I have the book here if you want it."

He suddenly looks angry and worried and shakes his head. "I am sorry Bella but you need to go away with him as planned. Take the notebook and I am sure that he will use it this weekend. Don't stop him as you may put yourself in danger. However he mustn't complete the task. If he does it will cause major damage. He needs all the codes for it to work. Once he starts we can swoop in and with all of the evidence charge him before he achieves his aim. This will limit the damage he causes."

I can't take it all in and look at him in dismay. "But how can I stop him?" Ben draws a small envelope from out of his jacket and says, "This is a sleeping drug. Put it in his drink and it will work almost instantly. It should buy us the time needed to get there before his task is completed. As soon as he is asleep I want you to get out of there. Leave everything, even the notebook and get as far away from him as possible. I will be monitoring you and I have one other form of protection for you." Handing me a phone he says, "This is on the same basis as before. Nobody knows that I have given it to you. You can call me if you need to; the number is programmed in already under Phoebe's name. Don't let anyone know you have it and only use it in an emergency. Nathan is extremely clever and will be able to suss it out if he knows about it." I take the phone and suddenly feel anxious, wondering if I can pull it all off.

Ben looks at me gently and once again desire races through me. I don't want to talk anymore. The need to be close to him is overwhelming. His eyes darken and I can hear his breathing intensify. He pulls me towards him and kisses me passionately. He holds on to me tightly and neither of us can bear to move apart. Reluctantly he pulls away. I realise that Phoebe will soon be back and say, "Does Phoebe know you are here?" He smiles gently and whispers, "Yes. She has been worried about you and contacted me. She arranged this so that we could talk." He laughs softly and looks at me raising his eyes, "Well, talking is overrated in my opinion." I blush and say, "Does she know anything?" Shaking his head he says, "No. She is just being a good friend. Don't tell her anything. It won't be long now and then we can pick up the pieces."

I watch him as he turns off the TV and the taps. He unlocks the door and then places the necklace around my neck again. Kissing me gently on the lips he tucks it underneath my top.

We hear footsteps outside and he whispers, "You had better go out and meet her. I love you Bella, I am with you so don't worry. Just keep safe, it won't be long now." I cling on to him loathe to let him go. The footsteps get nearer and there is a hesitant knock on the door. I pull away and open the door and slip outside. I don't look back. It's time to finish it.

Chapter 29

Phoebe looks guiltily at me as I leave the room. "I'm sorry B, you didn't mind that I asked Ben to come and meet you do you?" Smiling happily at her I give her a big hug. "Don't be silly Phoebs. You did what you thought was right. I love you for it." She looks at me with curiosity and says, "Well, what happened?" Looking down I sigh and say, "We talked and he explained a few things. He is going to give me some space to sort things out." Phoebe still looks anxious and says, "Did you tell him that you were spending time with Nathan?" Nodding I say, "Yes, I told him that I was with Nathan this weekend." Phoebe looks shocked and says, "How did he take it, was he angry?" Shaking my head I say, "No, he understood that it was something that I had to do." As I speak I choose my words carefully. I don't want to lie to her and the words that I have spoken are the truth, just in a different context to the one she is thinking of. I can't

wait to tell her the real story.

As we walk outside for lunch I ask her, "Why did you call Ben, Phoebe?" She blushes and says, "Because I don't think that it's right that you haven't talked about what Nathan said. You have been spending a lot of time with Nathan and to my knowledge you haven't even spoken to Ben on the phone. I am not silly Bella and know you extremely well. I know that you love Ben. Whatever is going on with Nathan though is a mystery to me. I just thought that if you saw each other you could work it out."

I smile gratefully at her. "I love you Phoebs. You're a good friend."

Over lunch I ask her about married life and how she is finding it. I need to divert the attention away from me and I enjoy hearing about her life as a married woman. She appears to have adjusted to it quite well and it helps that Boris is so easy going. "What's happening with the move?" I ask, remembering that they will be moving to their new house shortly. She pulls a face and says, "It's been held up because one of the chain has some problems with their sale. It's a real nuisance but at least it means that we can keep an eye on you for a bit longer." I laugh and she raises her eyes up at me.

Over coffee Phoebe broaches the subject of my birthday. "What are your plans for your birthday Bella. We could do something together or with some friends if you want?" I blush and suddenly feel very awkward.

"Nathan has asked me to go away with him and Bradley and Tina for my birthday." Phoebe looks aghast and I feel terrible. "Bella, please tell me you're not going? You can't get back with him, it's too soon." I know that I must be as red as a tomato and I hate lying to her. "It's not like that. We are going as friends. I was backed into a corner and didn't know how to say

no." Phoebe purses her lips and looks disapproving. "You know Bella, you are giving him the wrong impression. He is probably thinking that by Sunday evening you will be a couple again." She looks at me intently and I blush again. Her face changes and a look of horror comes over it. "Oh no, please don't tell me that you will be? You can't get back with him, please say you won't." I am actually quite surprised at her reaction. From what I can remember she loved Nathan and to everyone else he appears to be the injured party in all this. "Why not Phoeb's," I say looking at her carefully, "You always loved Nathan, what's changed?" She flushes and looks annoyed. "I know I did but something changed. I saw a different side to you when you were with Ben. Despite our misgivings you seemed to belong together. He obviously adores you and probably went about everything the wrong way but something inside me is telling me that it isn't Nathan that you are meant to be with, but Ben."
I can't believe what I am hearing. Phoebe has unwittingly hit the nail on the head. She sees me looking at her in surprise and blushes. "Anyway Bella, let's just go and get our lunch and forget about the men in your life." She grins at me and I laugh. She's right, it will be good to try and forget about them both for an hour at least.

The rest of the week passes fairly quickly; the weekend soon comes and my nerves are near breaking point. Nathan calls me a couple of times but thankfully I don't see him which I am relieved about. I spend some time at my parents and they are overjoyed that I am spending my birthday with Nathan - if only they knew! The night before I am due to go away Phoebe and Boris treat me to a night out for my birthday. We are going to the cinema and then on for dinner at my favourite restaurant. Just before we leave Boris looks at me anxiously. "I don't have to come if you would rather it was just the two of you." Phoebe raises her eyes up and I laugh, going over and hugging him. "Of course I want you to come. You are just as much a friend as Phoebe is and I can't think of a better way to spend it than with you both." He blushes and Phoebe and I giggle at his obvious discomfort. Before we go I open their present that they have given me. It is a lovely photograph of me and Phoebe in a silver frame. We are both laughing and look so happy. I hug them both. "I love it, thank you." Phoebe laughs and says, "That's not everything Bella. I have arranged for us both to go to Willington Spa for a pamper weekend, just us. You can choose when but that's as much input as you get. I have chosen the full experience and we can expect to feel totally spoilt by the end of it." I look at her in amazement. "This must have cost you both a fortune, it's too much." They laugh at me and Boris says, "Don't feel bad about it Bella, it's just as much for Phoebs as it is for you. You are the excuse she needed to book it. The good thing about it is that I will get to go away with my friends for the weekend too so we are all happy." We all laugh and the sight of Phoebe's excited face makes me grin at her. They are such good friends and I realise that unwittingly they have hit on the perfect gift for me. I am sure that by the end of this weekend I will be in need of a relaxing getaway.

Chapter 30

The morning soon comes and I get up bright and early to pack. My heart feels heavy and there are butterflies in my tummy as I think about what lays ahead. I hide the sleeping drug and mobile phone in a jumper in my case and hope that they remain undetected. I wonder if I will need them. Nothing may happen after all.

As I look at my Christmas book I wonder how something so inconsequential can be so important. I am not sure how he will use it and what will happen when he does. I remember Ben's warning to not let Nathan finish using it. I am not sure what I can do to stop him. What will happen if the sleeping drug doesn't work? As I sit on my bed I ponder the problem. Flicking through the pages in the book an idea begins to form in my mind. I realise that I will need to think several steps ahead as I can't risk failure. I know that there is something here that holds the key to Nathan's computer codes, but I don't know what. The book is made up of various lists. I think back to the evening at Bradley and Tina's and remember Nathan explaining that I have a Christmas card list

that remains the same and I just add to it if necessary. Looking at the list I see the familiar names and addresses of friends and family. Some addresses have been changed as people move and some names have been amended as people's partners change. I try to think as if I am in Nathan's shoes. What never changes from one year to the next? Surely his whole programme can't be based upon this? For all he knew I could have changed something and then it would disrupt things. I continue to look, trying to see anything that may help me. I must have sat here for some time because there is soon a knock at the door and I realise that Nathan has arrived. Jumping up I stuff the book into my bag and go to answer the door. However Phoebe reaches it before me and as I enter the living room I can see Nathan standing with Phoebe. I can tell that she is uncomfortable and I wonder why she has suddenly grown so unsure of him. They used to get along really well and it surprises me that she is so awkward with him now. As he sees me his face lights up and he crosses the room towards me. "Happy Birthday baby. You're looking great." He lifts me up and spins me around and then hugs me tightly to him. I can see Phoebe frowning at us and blushing say, "Put me down Nathan. You're embarrassing me." He laughs and drops me and turns towards Phoebe. "Nothing new there then hey Phoebs?" He winks at her and she smiles thinly at him. As she looks at me I can see the questions in her eyes. I look down, not wanting to face her scrutiny. This is all going be difficult enough without worrying about what she thinks. Nathan laughs saying, "Are you ready baby. Where's your bag and I'll carry it for you?"

"I'll just get it, I won't be a minute." Scurrying back

to my room I quickly throw the rest of my things in the bag. I jump as I hear the door open and look with some relief as I see Phoebe enter the room. She looks at me with a concerned expression and says, "Are you sure about this B? It just feels as if something is wrong and I can't put my finger on it." As I look at her I am once again amazed at her powers of perception. If she knew the real reason for the trip she would probably lock me in my room and call the police. I smile reassuringly at her. "It's fine Phoebs. If I'm honest I really need this weekend to sort things out properly once and for all. I suppose it is make or break really and is something that I need to do." Seeing her worried face I hug her saying, "I'll be fine, don't worry. We are going with Bradley and Tina and I will perfectly safe with them as chaperones." She smiles weakly but I can tell that she is not convinced.

We head back outside and Nathan smiles and takes my bag from me. "Thanks for this Bella; I am going to make this the best weekend that you have ever had. Nothing will be too much trouble and by the end of it you won't ever want to leave me again." I daren't look at Phoebe and just smile saying, "Come on then. Let's get going." As we start towards the door Phoebe says, "Oh Nathan, where are you going? I need the details in case of an emergency." I feel him stiffen beside me but his expression gives nothing away. I look at him questioningly and he looks sheepishly at us and says, "Marsden Grange actually." I look at him in shock and Phoebe looks bewildered. "Isn't that the place that you went with Ben and Melissa?" she says in surprise.

Nathan looks at me with a worried expression and I say, "Why there Nathan? We don't have the best of memories from that place." He flushes and says, "That's precisely why I chose it. That was when things went wrong for us baby and I have regretted it ever since. All I wanted to do was to rewind the clock and go back to that time and change what happened. I suppose this is my way of trying to do just that."
My eyes fill up, but not for the reasons that he must be thinking. That is my special place with Ben. The thought of going there with Nathan is unbearable. I don't want my happy memories of the place tainted by him and I would rather go anywhere else than there. He looks at me with concern and says, "Don't cry Bella. I am determined to put things right between us. We will make happier memories there that will drive the bad ones away. Let me do this and then we can truly move on?" Phoebe looks at him angrily and I just shrug and say, "Whatever. Come on Nathan, let's just get going." I turn and hug Phoebe and she clings onto me and whispers "Don't go Bella. Something isn't right, I can feel it." I squeeze her and say softly, "I'll be fine, don't worry. I will call you when I get there ok?" She nods but I can feel her disapproval following me all of the way to the car.
Before we start off Nathan turns to me and says, "Oh I nearly forgot. Did you remember the Christmas book that Tina wanted to look at?" He says it very matter of fact but I can see that his expression has tightened and there is an urgent look in his eyes. I maintain a blank look and say, "Oh yes, I did remember although I can't

imagine why she wants to see it really. I mean there is nothing that interesting in there after all." He smiles and I can see the relief in his eyes. "Oh I don't know, you girls and your weird ways. At least it will stop her from going on about it." I laugh and then decide to annoy him a bit more. "It's funny but I nearly didn't have it at all." Once again his expression briefly changes to one of alarm and he says, "What do you mean?" I can see that his hands have tightened on the steering wheel and I reply, "Well I left it lying around and when I looked for it I couldn't find it. I just remembered at the last minute and when I asked if anyone had seen it Phoebe told me that she had thought that it was nothing important and had used it to take to work for a meeting. Goodness knows what rubbish she wrote in it, although she assured me that she had just torn the pages out that she needed when she returned it but I am sure there were some pages missing." Suddenly there is tension in the air and I risk looking at Nathan with what I hope is an innocent expression. His knuckles are now white on the steering wheel and I can see a pulse working in his jaw, which I know to be a sign that he is stressed. He maintains a composed expression and smiles weakly at me saying, "Well let's hope that she didn't tear anything out that's important." He hesitates and then says, "Well if she did it probably wouldn't matter as it would have more than likely only been the last page. If I remember rightly that section was the present list. I would have thought that the most important list is the Christmas card one as that has the names and

addresses of all your friends and family. That is the one that you need the most. In fact hearing this makes me even more sure that you should let me input it all onto your computer. I will do that for you this weekend and I won't take no for an answer."
I sit in silence contemplating what he has just said, my mind going into overdrive.
As I look out of the window I suddenly notice with surprise that we are not heading towards Bradley and Tina's but straight onto the A3 heading south. Turning to Nathan I say, "I thought that we were picking up Bradley and Tina?" He smiles and says, "They are going to meet us there. Bradley had to work late yesterday and they may not make it until much later."
I feel extremely put out. The thought of being with Nathan on my own disturbs me and I can only hope that they arrive sooner rather than later.
Nathan spends the journey chatting about our past. He asks me about my family and what I have been up to. He doesn't mention Kinghams or Ben and it feels strange that they are not mentioned as they are both major factors in my life. My senses are on red alert and I notice that he is asking me about various people on my list, asking if certain people are still together or if anyone has moved. I try to make a mental note about who he mentions as they may hold the key to his success. By the time we pull into Marsden Grange I

feel emotionally drained.
As I take in the familiar surroundings I feel a huge lump form in the pit of my stomach. The last time that

I was here, Ben and I made love for the first time and found each other at last. We had been so happy and I had felt protected and loved at a time that I needed it the most. Looking over at Nathan who is walking back to the car after having checked in I wish with all my heart that it is Ben who is here instead of him. I feel the necklace against my bare skin and take comfort in the fact that he is close to me and now knows where Nathan has taken me. I wonder if he will come here. I know that he told me to get out once Nathan had taken the sleeping potion but I am still not sure what that would involve. Would he be waiting for me or would I just drive away getting as much distance between us as possible?

Getting into the car Nathan grins at me and says, "Ready baby. This is certainly going to be a weekend to remember." I smile and know in my heart that he is right; I just hope that everything goes according to plan.

Chapter 31

As we enter the lodge I take in the familiar surroundings. It is like coming home and as I look around images of Ben are everywhere. I take comfort from that and resolve not to let Nathan taint my memories of that special time with Ben. I wonder what will happen about the sleeping arrangements and as if by telepathy Nathan reads my mind. He looks at me sheepishly and says, "We'll take the larger room this time, Bradley and Tina can have our old room." I look at him in alarm and he crosses the room and takes my hands in his. "Don't worry Bella, I won't pounce on you. I know that it's not ideal but I am sure that we can at least share the bed as friends without anything happening. I promise to respect your boundaries and if it gets too awkward I will sleep out here on the settee."

He doesn't give me the chance to reply and says, "Anyway, let's get the fire going and make some drinks. We can go out to eat later to that pub we found when the others get here. You can unpack and then we can just chill out before they arrive."

Leaving him to it I head off to the room to unpack. I stuff the jumper concealing the phone and sachet underneath my other clothes in the drawer and then arrange my toiletries in the bathroom. Whilst I am absorbed in this I don't notice that Nathan has entered the room. I suddenly feel him behind me and it makes me jump. He reaches out to steady me and smiles at me softly. He is so close and I can feel his breath on my face. The bathroom is not very big and I am backed into the corner. He reaches up and runs his fingers down my face saying, "You are so beautiful baby. When I lost you it made me realise just how much I love you. This last year has been the worst of my life but seeing you standing here it is like it all never happened. You should now be my wife and we would be living the dream." His eyes pull me in and I am frozen to the spot. He pulls me closer to him and leans towards me. He cups my chin with his hands and brushes his lips lightly against mine. He then kisses me very gently and lightly. He pulls away and I can see the passion in his eyes.

Ruefully he says, "I am sorry I shouldn't have done that. You wanted space and I promised it to you and almost immediately went back on it. Please forgive me baby. You can trust me, I won't try anything on I promise." Finding my voice at last I say, "You shouldn't have done that Nathan. How can I trust what you say if you don't back up your words with actions. Please don't kiss me again or I will have to insist that you take me home." Stepping back he grins like a naughty schoolboy. "Come on; let me make it up to you. I want to give you your birthday present." I look at him surprise. "You didn't have to buy me anything Nathan." He laughs, "Of course I did. Let me spoil you baby. Nothing gives me greater pleasure than seeing you happy."

He pulls me into the bedroom and I notice a large box has been placed on the bed, beautifully wrapped with a big white ribbon holding the wrapping in place. Nathan looks excited and says, "Open it Bella, hurry up." Laughing I reach over and lift the parcel up. It feels fairly heavy and as I tear off the paper I am amazed to see the latest laptop computer. It must have cost him a fortune and I look at him stunned. "I can't accept this, this is too much." He laughs. "Nothing is too much for you baby. I can afford it and I only want the best for you. Let me set it up for you and I will make sure that everything you need is on there by the time we go home. Oh and whilst I am at it I will transfer your contacts on from your book if you like?" I look at him carefully and despite the light hearted way that he said it I now realise the real reason for the gift. Laughing I say, "Ok, but not now. Let's just settle in first and then go for a walk. It's too nice to spend the day inside on a computer. That can all wait until much later." I see him tense but then he smiles and says, "Whatever you want. It's your birthday and I aim to please."

I manage to stall him for a few hours and we go for a nice walk taking in the surroundings. I use the time to plan how I can stop him from completing his task. I had been relying on Bradley and Tina to distract him and this was all happening much faster than I had thought it would.

When we return to the lodge I notice with a sinking feeling that Bradley's car is still not there. Turning to Nathan I say, "Should you call Bradley to see where they are? We will be going out to eat soon and need to know when they will be arriving." Nathan nods and takes out his phone. After a few rings Bradley answers. They have a brief conversation and Nathan puts the phone away and says, "They're not coming until tomorrow morning. Bradley wasn't feeling well so they have decided to postpone their journey until he feels better."

He obviously notes the dismay on my face and says, "Don't worry Bella; we can still have a good time. We will go out to eat and then when we return I can sleep in their room and you will have your space." I relax slightly and smile saying, "Ok, let's go and get ready. All of that fresh air has made me famished." He nods and says, "Whilst you get ready I will make a start on your laptop." I smile and when I get to my room I close the door feeling suddenly very nervous. I realise that I am in too deep and want nothing more than to phone Ben and ask his advice. One good thing is that I still have the book so know that Nathan isn't going to be able to achieve anything without it. Taking the book I lock myself into the bathroom. Once again I flick through the pages and concentrate on the card list. I know that I don't have much time so decide to do the only thing that I can think of. I tear out the last two pages carefully. I don't want it to look obvious and if questioned I can blame Phoebe and act the innocent. I fold them up tightly and put them in my pocket. I know that I will need to hide them somewhere safe. I am not even sure if they are needed but feel that I have to try something. Quickly I put the book back and stuff the pages into the pocket of my jeans, intending to hide them later on.

Quickly I shower and get ready. Then once I am changed I head back outside the room to find Nathan, conscious of the missing pages burning a hole in my pocket.

As I enter the room Nathan looks up and smiles. "You look lovely Bella. I won't keep you long. I'll just finish up here and then get ready. I should only be about 20 minutes. Are you hungry?" Smiling I say, "Famished. It must be all of this fresh air." He laughs and says, "Why don't you make us a drink whilst you wait, it may help with the hunger pains?" Laughing I reply, "Do you want one?"

"Yes please, coffee would be great." He turns back to the computer and I set about making the drinks. Looking into the fridge I notice that we have forgotten the milk. "I'll just pop to the shop before it closes and grab some milk," I say heading towards the door. Nathan just waves his hand and I leave him to it. I am grateful to have some time on my own and as I start walking down the path once again my thoughts return to the last time that I was here. It feels so strange without Ben and I wish that he was with me. Suddenly I remember the phone and kick myself for not having thought of it sooner. I could phone Ben and ask for his advice. I think about going back for it but then realise that it may look odd. Nathan is bound to ask me what I forgot and I don't feel able to survive an inquisition. As I head towards the shop I think of the pages in my pocket. I need to hide them somewhere that Nathan won't think to look.

Soon I get to the shop and buy the milk. I think about giving them to the man in the shop to keep for me but decide that he would think me strange and if Nathan came with me he may mention them. On the way back I detour to find my favourite tree. Despite the fact that I am in a forest I will never forget where it is. I soon reach it and it feels as though I have found an old friend. Last time I was here Ben found me. It was then that we kissed and there was no going back after that. I think about how happy we were and how high we climbed. Leaning back against the trunk of the tree I think about my predicament. Turning the pages over in my hand I worry that they will be found. Suddenly in a flash of inspiration I think about the tree. Taking the milk out of the bag I place the pages into it and fold it up as small as I can. I walk around the tree to look for a possible hiding place. I concentrate on the area around the back of the tree and pull some of the leaves away. Using my hands I dig a small hole. The ground is soft and comes away easily. Placing the bag into the hole I brush some leaves over it and then look around for a marker. Spying a fairly large branch I place it over the leaves. It's a risk but keeping it on me is an even bigger one. Dusting the mud off my hands I grab the milk and slowly make my way back. I hope that it will be ok there. It shouldn't be for long with any luck and I pray that I am not around when Nathan finds out that they are missing.

Soon I get back to the lodge and as I go in I am relieved to see that Nathan has finished at the computer and hear him in the shower. Quickly I wash my hands and then make the drinks. I sit on the settee and wait for him. I feel so nervous and am sure that guilt must be written all over my face. As he comes into the room I gesture to his drink waiting on the side. Grabbing it he comes and sits next to me. "This is nice baby. Just like old times." He says smiling happily at me. I smile weakly and say, "Yes, it is rather. A lot has happened though this year, this time last year things were very different." He studies me and then looks at me regretfully. He runs his fingers through his hair and looks wistful. "I wish that I could turn the clock back. It all started here. I suppose that's why I wanted to come back. It's almost like I am trying to rewind time and hope that we could just carry on as before." As I go to speak he holds his hand up to stop me. "I know I mucked up baby. I have been paying for it ever since. I just want you to know that I regret it and know that even though you are here I have a long way to go before you will forgive me. I hope that you will one day." Putting the mug down he turns towards me and studies me intently. "After this weekend things may be different. I very much want us to be in each others lives but will respect whatever you want." I can see that he means every word and part of me feels sad for him. I do think that despite everything he does care for me. I can't help it and reach out to touch his hand. "I'm sorry too Nathan. You're right we were so happy this time last year. It wasn't all your fault though so please stop blaming yourself. Let's just leave all of that in the past where it belongs. I'm not saying that we can go back to how it was but I am glad that we are still friends." He squeezes my hand and I notice a sad look pass across his face. Then he grins and pulls me up. "Come on, let's go and eat."

Chapter 32

We had a lovely meal at the local pub. Nathan was good company and I felt quite relaxed sitting in the cosy pub. I suppose it was because we were away from the computer and the impending drama. I was just grateful for the respite and could have sat in there all night.

It is dark when we get back and Nathan decides to light the fire. I tease him, "Are you sure that you remember how, I mean you weren't that successful last time if I remember." He pushes me playfully and I leave him to it and go to rustle up some drinks.

We sip our drinks by the fire that is now roaring away and chat about people that we know. "Do you think that Bradley and Tina will come in the morning after all?" I say wondering if it's worth their driving down. Nathan smiles and says, "Of course they will come. They have been looking forward to it and if I know Tina she will drag Bradley out of his sick bed. She will be cross enough with him as it is." I smile and then say, "When we went to their house the other day she told me that she was lonely. Apparently she has lost touch with her old friends and the new ones are quite fake." Nathan looks at me with surprise. "I never knew that. She always seems so happy and settled in her new life. You would think that she has everything that she could ever wish for." Pulling a face I say, "Maybe materialistically but it would appear that even if you have everything that money can buy it still doesn't substitute having good friends." Nathan looks thoughtful and replies, "What about you, if you were in Tina's position do you think that you would be happy?" I shake my head. "No I wouldn't. Material things don't mean as much to me as friends and family. I would also have to work. I suppose it's easy to lose sight of what's important if you can have everything you want." Nathan smiles wryly and looking intently at me says, "What would you do if you had everything that money could buy, would you still do what you're doing now?" I look at him seriously. "Absolutely. I love my job and would hate to give it up. You shouldn't lose sight of what's important in life. You have to have a purpose, something to get up for in the morning and to strive for. I'm not saying that it wouldn't be nice to have everything you wanted in life but don't you think that life would get a bit boring after a while if everything was available to you all of the time." Nathan looks at me and I can tell that he is thinking of what I have said. Part of me wants him to wake up and stop what he is doing. I know that he is on a road to nowhere and wish that he would change his mind. The Nathan that I knew and loved was honest and caring. He was a good man and could have a wonderful life. I can tell that I have hit a nerve and we sit there together in silence, watching the flames of the fire dancing in front of us.

About an hour later I start yawning and Nathan laughs and says, "Off you go to bed Bella. You look done in." As I stand up I notice that he remains seated. "Are you off to bed too Nathan, you look tired as well?"
Nathan nods and says, "Yes, I think I will turn in. It's been a great day Bella, I have enjoyed it." He stands up and then to my surprise pulls me closer to him. He kisses me gently on the lips and says, "Happy Birthday baby. Sleep well. Thanks for coming here, it means a lot." My eyes fill with tears and I reply, "Thank you Nathan. It was kind of you to buy the present and take me for dinner. In fact this whole trip is very sweet. I hope that you sleep well."
Pulling away I head off to my room. He leaves me to it which I am grateful for. As I sit on my bed tears run down my face. I do love him and don't want him to pursue the course he has chosen. Even though I no longer love him in the way that I used to, I do love the Nathan that I fell in love with. He is not my soul mate like Ben but I care very much what happens to him. I want him to be happy and to find somebody who loves him back. As I get ready I wonder if I can steer him away from what he has planned. Maybe I can save him and he will abandon it? I feel as though I owe it to him to at least try. Obviously I can't let him know that I know but maybe if I can make him see that life is so much better living it honestly, then he can be saved.
I fall off to sleep and to my surprise wake up quite late the next day. At first I am not sure where I am and then it all comes flooding back. I get up and quickly get ready. When I reach the living room I am amazed

to see that it is empty. I wonder if Nathan is still asleep. The computer is still where he left it and everything looks the same. I decide to make myself a cup of tea and wonder if I should make one for Nathan and take it in for him. Once the tea is made I decide that I will and cautiously open his bedroom door. I can see that he is still in bed sleeping soundly. Smiling to myself I tiptoe back out. He obviously needs the rest and I am glad that he has slept. Hopefully I still have enough time to steer him away from his plan.

I decide to go for a walk. I don't want to disturb him so head off towards the shop. This time I remember to take the phone. I want to phone Ben, it is suddenly really important that I speak to him. I want his advice and the thought of hearing his voice makes my heart leap.

As I walk through the woods I decide that it's best if I phone him when I am some distance away and out of sight and hearing of anyone. Excitedly I press the contact name and hear the phone ringing. He answers it almost immediately and I almost weep with relief when I hear his voice. "Bella, are you ok?" His voice is husky and full of concern. Biting my lip I contain the tears that are threatening to fall. "I miss you Ben, I'm sorry but I had to call you." I hear his sharp intake of breath and he says, "I miss you too and the thought of you there with him is unbearable."

"I know, but I'm ok. I just wanted to tell you where we are and what has happened." He speaks softly and says, "I know where you are and I know that he hasn't started inputting the codes. We are not far away and rest assure we are looking out for you and if we think that you are in any danger I will come for you."

I am surprised and look around me, half expecting to see him watching me from a tree or something. "I love the fact that you are near Ben. I wish that I could see you. Please tell me that this will be over soon?"

"I hope so Bella. I want you safely back with me where you belong."

His words give me the comfort and strength that I need. "Ben, can I ask you a question?" He sounds surprised and says, "Of course you can, what do you need to know?" With a deep breath I say, "If Nathan doesn't use the codes and carry out his plan, would he be in the clear?" There is a short silence and then Ben replies in a low voice. "I know where you are going with this Bella. I heard what you said to him last night and you are probably thinking that you can save him." I am amazed at how quickly he understands the situation. He always seems to know what I am thinking and I suddenly remember that he can hear everything we say, via the necklace. This comforts me and makes me feel protected. He carries on with a sombre tone to his voice. "Bella. I love the way that you think that everything is so black and white. To answer your question, no Nathan would not be in the clear. This is just one of many things that he has been involved in and the case is stacking up against him quite considerably. We are only involved if the crime becomes extremely serious. Regardless of whether or not he executes his plan, when he is caught he is due a lengthy prison term." His voice softens and he says, "I

am sorry, I know that you want to think the best of him but it is too late for him. As I said before, don't underestimate him. You need to get out of there as soon as possible. He wouldn't think twice about you if he thinks we are on to him. Use the sleeping powder and get out. We will do the rest. Once he is asleep take his car and drive as far away from there as you can. Please it is important that you understand the gravity of the situation. Nathan is not who you think he is."
I feel shocked at his words. Tears come into my eyes thinking of Nathan and what he has become. Brushing them away I whisper, "Ok, thanks Ben. I love you." There is a short silence and then he answers me huskily and I can feel his emotion radiating through the phone. "I love you too Bella, please take care. I would never forgive myself if anything happened to you." I nod as though he can see me and then end the call. With an extremely heavy heart I head towards the shop.

Chapter 33

Armed with enough bacon and eggs to feed a small army I return to the lodge. On the way back I think about what I have to do. As soon as Nathan starts inputting the codes I will make him a drink. Once he is asleep I will take his car and drive to Ben's. It is the only place that I can think of to go to where I will be safe.

On entering the lodge I can see that Nathan has woken up and is sitting at the computer. He looks up and smiles. "Morning Baby, you're up bright and early. Did you sleep well?" Smiling back at him I reply, "Yes thank you. I made you a cup of tea earlier but you were sound asleep so I went to the shop for breakfast supplies." Getting up he comes over. I can feel him studying me and I don't know why but I feel

unnerved. Reaching out he takes the bag from my hands. "Here, let me take that from you." Placing the bag on the counter he then comes over and stands directly in front of me. He looks at me as though

searching for something.

Feeling a bit awkward I say, "Have you heard from Bradley and Tina today? I could hold off making breakfast until they arrive if they are nearly here." Shaking his head he says, "No, I haven't."

He reaches out and pulls me towards him. Instantly I

stiffen up which doesn't go unnoticed and I see his eyes narrow. Stroking my hair he buries his face in my hair and inhales sharply. "You smell so good Baby, you always did." I can feel him crushing me to him and can hear his heart beating rapidly. Pulling back he leans towards me and kisses me deeply and passionately. Shocked I try to pull away but he is too strong and my mind races away, trying to think of how I can extricate myself from this situation. He pulls me even closer and his kisses get more urgent. He is holding me in such a way that I can't move and I am powerless in his grasp. Finally he pulls back and groans, "Come on baby, it's time that we moved this on. I have waited long enough and know that we were meant to be together. I know that you want it too, otherwise you wouldn't have come." He runs his fingers underneath my top and I can feel the contact on my bare back.

I look at him in horror and push against him. "Nathan no! You've got this all wrong."

Pulling back he looks at me his eyes hardening. Suddenly fear runs through me at the situation that I am now in. His eyes narrow a fraction and then he smiles ruefully. Releasing me he moves away. He runs his fingers through his hair and as he looks back at me I notice that his face looks remorseful. "I'm sorry baby. I thought that you wanted me too. It's ok, I get the message." Shaking I just stand here not knowing what to say. Looking past him I suddenly notice the notebook lying next to the computer and realise that he has been entering the codes whilst I have been out.

Seeing me Nathan smiles. "Sorry, I hope you don't mind but when I went looking for you this morning I noticed the book and thought that I would make a start whilst you were out." Shrugging my shoulders I try to look non committal. "That's ok. Listen Nathan, I'm sorry that I reacted like that just now. It took me by surprise. Why don't I make us breakfast whilst you carry on and then when Bradley and Tina arrive we can all go out." Nathan smiles. "That sounds good." He goes to sit down but then turning around says, "I'm sorry Bella. I won't try anything on again. It's up to you now. You know where I am when you feel ready, I will wait for you." Once again he looks intently at me and feeling myself blushing I say, "I'll just go and use the bathroom and then I'll be back to make breakfast." Racing to my room I quickly close the door behind me. I can feel my heart racing. I need to get some distance from Nathan. Something is bothering me. The atmosphere is different somehow, more intense and foreboding. I wonder if it's because of my conversation with Ben.

Sitting on the bed I try to gather my thoughts. I run through the events of the morning in my mind and then I think about the book. Nathan has been in my room this morning. He must have come looking for me, as I did him. This is not the problem though. He says that he saw the book and took it to begin working on it; however I know that the book was hidden in my drawer. Therefore he must have searched for it. I am not surprised as after all that is the reason why we are here.

Going over to the drawer I search for the sleeping powder. I find the envelope where I left it and thank my lucky stars that he didn't find it. My heart thumping, I stuff it into my pocket. I know that this is the time to use it. It won't take him long to achieve his task and I must stop him before he realises that some of the pages are missing.

Taking a deep breath I go back to the living room. As I enter the room I am surprised to see that Nathan is not at the computer, but working away in the kitchen. Smiling at me he says, "Here you go baby, I made you a drink. You must be desperate for one after your early morning walk." He pushes a steaming mug of tea towards me. "Sit down; the breakfast can wait for a minute. I just had a text from Bradley. They are about 30 minutes away so we can wait for them."

Reaching for the mug my mind starts racing. This will make it more difficult now. If they are here it will be difficult to give him the sleeping powder and make my escape. I only have 30 minutes to execute the plan, otherwise it could all go wrong. Nathan comes and sits beside me. Nervously I sip my tea and I can feel him watching me intently. "You seem nervous baby." He says gently, probing me with his eyes. "I feel as though it's my fault. I shouldn't have pounced on you like that." Grinning ruefully he runs his fingers through his hair. "I never could keep my hands off you could I?" Laughing softly he clinks his mug to mine. "I would like to propose a toast. To us Bella and whatever the future may bring, good or bad, may we always be together."

I smile feeling somewhat relieved at his change of demeanour. Clinking my mug against his we drink our tea, looking out at the forest. As we sit there side by side, I try to think about how I can do this. Seeing that he has finished I say, "Would you like another drink Nathan, I think that I will?" Quickly finishing my drink I stand up and reach for his mug. He looks at me with a soft expression. "Why not, you make it and I will sort out your computer and then when the others arrive it will be finished." As he hands the mug to me his fingers brush against mine. He smiles, but I notice for the first time that his smile doesn't reach his eyes. They have a hard look to them and I can feel him watching me as though he is waiting for something. Stumbling away I head for the kitchen. As I go though I suddenly feel strange. The room starts to spin and my legs turn to jelly. The last thing I remember is a pair of strong arms catching me as I fall back.

Chapter 34

My head is pounding and my throat is dry. As the room spins into view I try and remember where I am. I appear to be lying in bed. It all seems strange and foggy and I can't remember what happened. Glancing over I notice that the clock says 5pm. Goodness I must have slept all day.

Shifting over I try to sit up but then fall back down again as I realise that my limbs have turned to jelly. I feel drained and have no strength in me at all. The blood rushes to my head and I try desperately to remember what happened. The last thing I can remember is going to make the drinks and then nothing. In alarm I reach up and with a sinking feeling notice that my necklace is gone. In fact I have nothing on at all. Suddenly I feel sick. Nathan must have put me to bed and removed my clothes. Tears spring to my eyes at the thought of what may have happened. Surely he wouldn't have tried anything on. It doesn't feel as though he has but then again what do I know, I have been out for hours.

Before I can think of anything else the door opens and I see Nathan standing in the doorway. He looks at me angrily and I suddenly feel very afraid. He approaches me menacingly and I don't recognise the man standing in front of me. His face has hardened and his eyes flash at me angrily. I look wildly around and with a sinking feeling realise what a dangerous situation I am in. He sits on the side of the bed and I shrink back away from him. "Awake at last," he says, and his tone is menacing. "Nathan, what's going on, why am I naked in bed and how did I get here?" His laugh sends chills through me. "So many questions, but before I answer them I have a few of my own." I grab the covers to me and look at him in alarm. He speaks in a cold voice that I don't recognise as coming from him. "Do you know what Bella; something has been puzzling me for quite some time. Why would you willingly spend time with me over the last couple of weeks when you have just broken up with your boyfriend, who you chose over me in such a public fashion?" I blush as he looks at me sharply, probing my face with his eyes. "It also puzzled me that to my knowledge you never heard from him or contacted him in that time and your belongings were returned the very next day. Doesn't that strike you as odd too?" I shift nervously and avoid looking at him. He grabs my wrist sharply and I wince at the sudden pain. "You can't bear me to touch you and appear to be going through the motions of something, but it is obvious that you would rather be anywhere else but with me." I shake my head, trying to clear it from the fog that occupies it still. "No Nathan, you've got it all wrong. I just feel as if I owe it to you to try and see if there is still anything between us." He laughs derisively. "Is that really the best you can do? I always knew you were stupid and still you don't disappoint. It's why I chose you in the first place. Dear trusting, gullible

Bella. God you're so boring. The last two years have been the dullest of my life." Feeling the full force of his venomous words I recoil in shock. Trembling I say, "What do you mean, I don't understand?" He laughs and it sounds hollow and brittle. "Even now I have to spell it out. Well here goes. I needed someone as gullible as you for my plan to work. I took the job at Kinghams as a cover for a much larger project that I had in mind. I watched you for a while and found out all I could on you before I engineered your computer problems. I needed a fall guy, someone who wouldn't guess what I was up to. Someone to take the blame when the time came. You were perfect. You fell for my charms and I used you. It was easy to make you fall in love with me. I enjoyed your company to a degree even though it lacked a certain sort of stimulation, if you know what I mean."

Tears run down my face. I can't take it all in. I never thought for one minute that the whole thing had been a lie. He carries on relentlessly. "It was all going to plan and then Ben Hardcastle took over. He started to interfere with things. I could tell that you had a history and he kept on making me do other things at Head Office, taking me away from my valuable work at Kinghams. It wasn't all bad though because he introduced me to Melissa." His tone changes and his face softens. "Now there is a woman equal to me in everything. Our attraction was instant. She is a goddess, everything a man could wish for. Funny, beautiful, intelligent, in fact my soul mate in every way. She is like a drug to me. I couldn't stay away and

it drove me mad that there was everything I had ever wished for but I still had to see things through with you." I feel sick as the realisation hits me that everything in my life has been built on a lie for the last two years. Tears run down my face but I don't wipe them away. It is all too much to take in. In a shaky voice I say, "If you felt like that Nathan why didn't you just let it go and start again?" His laugh cuts through me. He sounds bitter and angry and I almost can't look at him as he carries on. "If it was that easy don't you think I would have? No it had gone too far. Everything was set in place and then Melissa got pregnant. It all unravelled from then on. All I needed was your stupid notebook to put the plan in action. I hadn't banked on your falling for Ben Hardcastle. I couldn't get near you or the notebook and I needed you both for my plan to work. To make matters worse Melissa took off and I couldn't find her. I was devastated. I looked for her everywhere but she was nowhere to be found. I had lost everything."
Looking at Nathan I still can't take it all in. What he is telling me is the last thing that I thought I would hear. "So are you telling me that everything since you met me has been a set up? What about your parents, were they in on it too?" I can feel myself getting angry and Nathan laughs. "Of course not. They know nothing. I had it all worked out. You were my fall guy and would take all of the blame. I would have been devastated at your criminal ways and everyone would have felt sorry for me. Not that I intend to hang around to find out. My life is already mapped out for me far away

from this country. All I need is the final set of codes and then I will be gone." Suddenly he looks at me angrily again and snaps, "When you came in to my room this morning I was already awake. I pretended to be asleep and when I heard you leave I searched your room for the book. Interestingly enough though the book wasn't the only thing that I found." I shift anxiously wondering what he is talking about. It couldn't have been the phone because I had that with me."

He carries on bitterly, "Imagine my surprise when I found an envelope of some sort of drug secreted amongst your clothes. I asked myself, why would Bella have this? She doesn't do drugs and hardly even drinks. It made me think and then everything started to fall into place. You were here with an ulterior motive. This was your insurance policy and I was the intended victim." He laughs once again and it sounds hollow. "I emptied the contents into a mug and replaced the envelope. When you came back I made you the drink and watched with interest what would happen next. It was soon obvious that it was a strong sedative. Then I started to think about who had given it to you and why? You are not clever enough to have worked everything out for yourself so I knew that someone else was feeding you information. It didn't take a genius to work out who and it made me think about the fact that despite my best efforts I could never find anything out about Ben Hardcastle."

Nathan laughs again and looks at me saying, "It appears that I wasn't the only one using you Bella darling. To be duped once is unfortunate, but twice, that is just plain stupid." Tears sting my eyes once again. Swallowing hard I refuse to believe that Ben was using me.

Suddenly Nathan stands up. He grabs some clothes and throws them at me. "Anyway, as nice as it is to chat to you I would like to bring this charade to an end. Whilst you were sleeping I entered the codes and had intended on being long gone before you woke up. The trouble is there is a page missing. As it turns out it is quite a vital one and I need it to finish the job. The reason that you have nothing on is because I couldn't trust the fact that you didn't have some sort of surveillance device on. So get dressed Baby and go and get the page and then I will be out of your hair." Grabbing the clothes I quickly put them on, taking the time that they have given me to work out what my next move should be.

As soon as I am dressed Nathan grabs my arm roughly and pulls me towards the door. "Where is it?" he hisses. "Nathan you're hurting me, let me go." I say angrily. He squeezes my arm harder and says, "I'll hurt you a lot more than this if I don't have that page in the next few minutes." Shaking my head I say, "I told you, Phoebe must have torn it out. It is probably long gone." Then to my surprise Nathan strikes me across the face with a resounding blow. I am taken by surprise and the shock sets in before the pain. He shouts, "Don't you lie to me, I have had enough. The pages were intact when we arrived. I checked when you were in the toilet. Only you could have removed it and I am not waiting any longer. If you don't get it for me now I will beat it out of you." Before I can say anything he delivers another blow sending me stumbling across the room. I cry out in pain as I slam against the wall. Before I can recover he grabs hold of me again and pulls my arm behind my back. I cry out in agony, my face throbbing from his punch. I can taste blood in my mouth.

Then out of nowhere the door flies open and I see Tina and Bradley enter the room. Tina looks at me in shock and cries, "Nathan, stop it, what are you doing?" He shouts back, "Stay out of this both of you. It's time Bella learnt who's boss around here. I have waited long enough and I am not going to wait any longer." Bradley looks at Tina and then at me with a worried expression. "Come on Nathan, this isn't helping. Bella will get the missing page, won't you?" Bradley looks at me anxiously and I can see Tina also looking at me with a worried expression. Bradley continues. "Let her go Nathan and let Tina talk some sense into her. Give them 5 minutes and then if she still won't cooperate you can do what you have to do." I can feel Nathan's grip loosen and then he releases me and pushes me away. "Ok, you have 5 minutes and then I won't be responsible for my actions." He leaves the room with Bradley in tow who closes the door behind them. Sinking to the floor I put my head in my hands. Tina rushes up to me and hugs me to her. "Bella, thank goodness we got here when we did. Are you ok?" I start to cry and just sit there not knowing what is happening. Tina pulls my face towards hers and I can see the anxiety in her expression. "Bella, Nathan isn't joking. We only have 5 minutes. You must get the missing page otherwise I cannot guarantee your safety. It's not worth it. Just give it to him and then we will be gone and you will be safe." I whisper, "It's not here. It's buried in the woods." Looking at me with determination Tina pulls me up on my feet. "I'll come with you. I won't let him harm you. Not long now and then you will be safe." Heading out of the room I flinch as I see Nathan standing by the door. He is unrecognisable as the Nathan that I knew. He looks at me in a threatening manner and Tina says, "Bella has hidden it in the woods. I will go with her and you two stay here and get ready to leave. Melissa is on her way and we haven't got long." Before they can reply Tina pushes me out of the door and closes it behind her. Taking my arm forcefully she propels me towards the forest. "Lead the way Bella, as I said, we don't have much time."

As we walk I say, "What did you mean that Melissa is coming?" Tina laughs and says, "Melissa is coming to drive us to the helicopter that is waiting to take us out of the country. Nathan couldn't bear to leave her behind and told her everything. The plan is that once we have the full set of codes we can finish the job on the way out of here." Stopping suddenly I say, "What about me, Nathan said that I would be the fall guy. If I give you the codes I would be setting myself up to take the blame?" Tina pulls me around angrily and I shrink back at the hard expression on her face. "For goodness sake Bella just get the missing page. This would have been over a long time ago if you hadn't started meddling in things you know nothing about. I for one have had enough and won't let you stall us for one minute longer than necessary. You will be ok if you cooperate. If you don't then I can't be held responsible for what Nathan may do. He is a dangerous man who doesn't care what he has to do to get what he wants as Sophie found out to her cost." Looking at Tina I can feel the shock very evident on my face. I stutter, "What do you mean, what happened to Sophie?" Tina's eyes narrow and she says, "Sophie was caught snooping through Nathan's things. He waited until he was sure that she had found out enough about him to incriminate him and then he struck." Feeling sick I say, "What do you mean, what did he do?"

"Well put it this way, she is currently in hospital recovering from a heroin overdose, not by her own doing I may add." I can't take it all in and my head starts spinning. Tina says harshly, "Listen Bella, we haven't got long. Give me the page and then I will tell you what to do."

By now we have reached the tree. Weighing it all up in my mind I decide to hand over the page. I have stalled for long enough and my priority now is to get out of the situation in one piece. I nod and say, "We are here now; it's buried at the foot of the tree." Racing over to the far side of the tree I begin to brush away the leaves from the piece of wood that I placed over the page. Tina waits impatiently, her eyes not leaving me for a second. It doesn't take long and I soon have the page in my hand. Standing up I hold it out to Tina. Quickly she holds out her hand and says, "Now give it to me, hurry up." As I hold out the page towards her she snatches it out of my hand, then looking urgently at me she says, "Now Bella, this is important. You mustn't come back with me. Nathan will not just leave you behind in one piece. I know that he has something planned for you and I can't be a party to it." I suddenly feel very afraid. I know that she is right and I feel sick at the thought of what he must have in mind. Tina carries on. "I want you to hit me as hard as you can across the face. It must leave a mark and then you must run as fast as you can away from here. Don't look back and don't go for help to the office or shop. They will not be able to protect you from him and it will be the first place that he looks." Shaking my head I say, "I can't hit you Tina, just let me run, I don't want to hurt you." Tina's replies angrily, "You must otherwise I could be in danger if he thinks that I let you go. Please Bella; do as I say for both our sakes. He will come after you, I can't stress enough how important it is that you hide. We don't have long, but for your own safety you have to do this." Nodding tears flow down my cheeks as I take a step backwards. Mustering all of my strength I land a hard blow across Tina's face. Her head snaps to the side and almost instantly I see her cheek turn red. Tears spring to her eyes and her breath comes in short, sharp gasps. She says huskily, "Run Bella, go now and don't look back. Don't come out until you are sure it is safe." Suddenly she hugs me and says softly, "Thank you Bella, I can't thank you enough for bringing this to an end." Then standing back she says urgently, "Now run and don't look back, and good luck."

Chapter 35

I start running and do as she says. I don't look back and just run trying to place as much distance as I can between us. My heart thumps in my chest and I am soon out of breath. My side starts to hurt but I carry on, deeper and deeper into the forest. I don't know where I am going but I know that I need to keep on. Soon I can't run anymore and look around me, taking in where I have ended up. It is getting dark and I realise that I am in the middle of nowhere. All I can hear is my own breath and heart thumping. Spying a suitable tree nearby I decide to climb it. My intention is to get as high as I can and hopefully see where I have ended up. Despite the darkness drawing in I manage to climb quite high. I can see above the trees and recognise the Lodges in the distance. Despite feeling that I have run for miles I can see that I have not gone far at all. I appear to have run in a large circle. I am not even sure how long I have been running for. I wonder if Nathan has started to look for me yet and hope with all my heart that Tina's story held up. Despite her involvement in Nathan and Bradley's plan, I do feel that her heart was in the right place. She seemed sad and lonely and I realise that life couldn't have been easy for her.

Suddenly I hear shouting in the distance. Straining to hear I recognise the sound of Nathan's voice calling my name. Shrinking back against the branch holding me I am grateful for the curtain of ivy that is screening me from view. Holding on tightly I try to stay as quiet as possible. I can hear him getting closer. Then I hear him shouting, "Bella, where are you? Come on baby it was only a joke. I didn't mean any of it, come out, it is getting dark now and I need to know that you are safe."

It feels as if he is so close now and I almost dare not breathe in case he finds me. I know that he is dangerous and believe nothing he says anymore. My thoughts turn to Ben. Where is he? He said that he was nearby. Surely he knows by now that something has gone wrong? He said that he would come and get me if things went wrong. What if Nathan was telling the truth and he had just been using me? I was duped once by Nathan which has brought my judgement into question. I would be destroyed if what he said turned out to be true. Through all of this Ben was the only one that mattered to me. I did this to protect him. With relief I hear Nathan's voice getting more and more distant and realise that he has moved away from the immediate area. I am not sure how long I will be able to sit in the tree. I start to shiver. The day's events are catching up with me and shock is beginning to set in as my mind processes the information. It is also getting cold and my hands are turning blue. After what seems like ages I hear a car approaching in the distance. After about 10 minutes I hear a horn blast out. I can't see what is happening and wonder if it is Melissa, come to pick them up. I think about where they may be heading to and if Ben and his bosses know to follow them. So many questions buzz around my mind. I am at a loss as to what to do now and decide to hold on as long as possible in the tree. All the time that I am up here nothing can happen to me. Nobody knows where I am and I am safe. If I venture down Nathan or Bradley may be waiting, and I think in horror of what they may have in store for me. Thinking of Sophie my heart hammers in my chest. The thought of what Nathan did to her is appalling. I may not be so lucky if he gets to me. At least she is safe now and getting the treatment that she needs. As I sit there thinking of everything I start to feel rain falling on my face. I know now that I will have to get down. If it rains too hard the tree will become slippery and I may fall. I listen carefully for the sound of anyone below, but all I can hear is the sound of the forest. I can't remember hearing if the car pulled away and for all I know it is still there. Carefully I start to climb down and try to be as quiet as I can. The rain is falling harder now and as I thought the branches are becoming slippery. After what seems like an eternity I jump down onto the forest floor below, the leaves crunching underneath my feet. Gingerly I move away from the direction of the lodges. I know that I am not safe yet and need to find a place to hide. The darkness is well and truly closing in and I realise that I may need to spend the night out here. Using the last rays of light I spy a clearing underneath a group of trees.

Dodging under the branches covering the entrance I sit as far in the shadows under the protective covering as I can. Hugging my knees up to my chest for added warmth I sit there in the darkness, waiting and listening for any sign that the danger has passed. I sit like this for what seems like hours. The only sounds that I hear are those of the forest. It is pitch black now and the rain is finding a path through the trees and is falling onto me, seeping through the thin layers of my clothes. My teeth start to chatter and I shiver with the cold. Still I can't move. Even if I did manage to get out of my hiding place I am not sure if I have the strength to go anywhere. The entire time my head is buzzing with what has happened. Nathan said that I was the fall guy. What did that mean? It is obvious that he has set something up to blame me for everything, but I am at a loss as to what it could be. Soon I feel my eyes closing. Fighting to stay awake, I know that I mustn't sleep. Despite the sanctuary it offers, the forest is now my immediate danger. If I don't move soon I will freeze to death or catch pneumonia.

Deciding that I should move I crawl out of my hiding place, dusting the leaves from my legs. They don't appear to be working very well at the moment and I struggle to put one foot in front of the other. Cautiously I make my way through the forest, straining to listen for any danger signs. I am so exhausted. If I wanted to move quickly I wouldn't be able to. Every few steps I stop to catch my breath. The cold is seizing control of my limbs and it is getting more and more difficult to move. I start to sob quietly. I am so scared. Scared of what may be lying in wait for me and scared of the predicament that I am in now. All I want is Ben and I am so worried that he doesn't want me. Suddenly I am aware of movement ahead of me. I can hear voices and see pinpricks of light coming through the trees. I can hear the barking of dogs and I am scared that it may be Nathan. I look around me wildly for somewhere to hide. I know that I don't have the strength to climb a tree so dodge behind a nearby tree and lean against it, as still as I can. The voices are getting nearer and the light stronger. I can hear my name being called and then a volley of barking. Then as if in slow motion I see a dog crash through the clearing, rushing towards me. I hear someone call, "Over here, there's something here." The light gets brighter and I hold my hands up to my eyes as the light blinds me. The voices are nearer and then I am aware of some people running towards me. I can't see their faces but then I hear his voice. "Bella, it's me Ben, you're safe now." Looking up I can see Ben rushing towards me, his face looking both worried and relieved at the same time. Reaching out to me I fall into his arms and that is the last thing that I remember.

Chapter 36

As if from a distance I can hear voices. It takes a little while for my mind to adjust itself and then I remember the events that have unfolded. In alarm I open my eyes and blink as an unfamiliar room swims into view. I try to sit up but then fall back as my body lets me down. I feel so weak and appear to have no strength left in me at all. Feeling a hand in mine I look across and see with considerable relief that Ben is slumped over the bed next to me, holding my hand tightly but obviously fast asleep as he sits in the chair next to my bed. As my eyes take in my surroundings I can see that I am in a hospital bed. There is nobody else here and the voices that I heard must have come from outside in the corridor for it is only the two of us here. As I look at Ben I feel so much love for him. I have missed him very much and seeing him sitting next to me is a huge relief. He is obviously exhausted and I can see that he is as dishevelled as I was. There is a generous amount of stubble on his face and his hair is tousled. His clothes have mud on them and he looks as if he has had them on for days. The door opens gently, interrupting my thoughts and I turn to see a nurse come into the room. She smiles at me as she sees that I am awake and then laughs gently as she sees Ben sleeping next to me. Indicating Ben she says in a whisper, "He has been so worried and won't leave your side. He will be glad to see that you are back with us." As she speaks he suddenly jerks awake and then realisation sets in and I see his eyes burning into mine with so much love that any doubts that Nathan has put in my mind about his feelings for me vanish immediately.

"Bella, thank God you're awake," he says, gripping my hand, the relief in his face evident. Tears spring into my eyes as I squeeze his hand weakly. My voice is husky and weak as I reply, "I love you Ben." He brings his other hand up and strokes my face. "I love you too Bella, thank God you are safe." The Nurse coughs discreetly and says, "I'm sorry guys but I need to check on Bella." Ben jumps back saying, "Of course, please go ahead Nurse. Do you need me to leave?" Shaking her head she replies, "No need, I just need to check her temperature and blood pressure, then I will let the Doctor know that she has come round." It doesn't take her long and then we are alone. I have so many questions but as I open my mouth to speak Ben puts his finger to my lips. "Hush Bella. I know that you have many questions but all of that can wait." Taking my hand again he looks lovingly at me. "It's over now Bella. You are safe now and back with me where you belong. The nightmare is over and all that matters now is that you make a full recovery. The Doctor said that you were suffering from exhaustion and the effects of the sleeping drug. You also have a mild case of Hypothermia. As soon as he discharges you I am taking you home."

Smiling at him I whisper, "Stop talking Ben. The only

thing I want is for you to kiss me." His face relaxes and lights up as the worried expression turns to one of happiness. He leans towards me and his hand slips gently behind my head. He pulls my face towards his and I feel his lips on mine. Softly, he kisses me and the feelings inside of me explode. I have missed his touch so much. He is all that matters to me, as long as I have Ben, I have everything.

The door opens again and we hear a man's voice say, "Put my patient down young man, goodness me whatever next." Laughing Ben releases me and we turn to see the Doctor watching us with a twinkle in his eye. "Good to see you back with us Bella; you have given this young man quite a shock." I smile weakly at him. He looks as if he is in his 50's and has a jovial face. I warm to him immediately. Approaching me he says, "You will probably be feeling very weak young lady but don't worry about it, it is just the effects of the medication. If your observations continue to be ok you can probably be released later on today. You just need bed rest for a few days whilst your body recovers. I can prescribe some medicine for the Hypothermia but I am pleased to say that there is no lasting damage and you should make a full recovery." Looking over at Ben he says, "Make sure that you look after her and don't let her do anything for a few days. Lots of hot drinks and TLC." Ben says falteringly, "Thank you Doctor. Don't worry I will take good care of her." The Doctor smiles and says, "I know you will. I will pop in later on today and then I am confident that I can release her to your care. Right,

I must be off, never enough hours in the day you know." Abruptly he leaves and Ben laughs as the door closes. Turning towards me he says, "I can't wait to get you home. Like the Doctor says, I intend to look after you, not just through your recovery but for many more years after that."

Sitting down Ben takes my hand in his and looks lovingly into my eyes. "You are everything to me Bella. This last couple of weeks have been the worst of my life. I would have done anything to stop you getting involved as my boss knew. It is why she met you behind my back." His expression turns grim. "I have left her in no doubt as to my feelings about that, however once you had left I made it my job to monitor you and keep you as safe as I could. When you went missing I was beside myself. There was no way of contacting or locating you and the thought of you out there in the forest all alone was driving me mad." Reaching towards him I stroke the side of his face. "I'm sorry Ben." I say weakly. "I had to stay hidden. Tina said that Nathan had something bad planned for me and I wasn't safe. I had to hide until I was sure the coast was clear." Ben's face changes to one of anger. "When I think of that man anywhere near you it makes my blood boil. He is evil and deserves everything that is coming to him." Seeing my expression Ben's face relaxes. "Anyway, enough about him. He can't hurt you anymore. I am sure that we will soon find out what has become of him." Surprised I say, "Don't you know Ben? I thought that you would by now." Squeezing my hand he says, "No, as soon as I found you nothing else mattered. I left him to everyone else and I haven't heard from anyone since. But don't worry, he won't have gotten far." Thinking about Nathan and what happened brings back many unpleasant memories. I can feel my body aching from the effects of his treatment of me and realise that I must look a complete mess. Turning to look at Ben I say, "Please can you help me up Ben, I need to go to the bathroom." Ben pulls back the covers and gently lifts me up out of bed. The feeling of being in his arms again is such a relief. I cling on to him as he carries me over to the bathroom. He puts me down and I hold on to the door handle for support. "Will you be ok in there?" he says, his voice worried. I nod, "Yes, I'll be fine. I'll call you if I need any help." I slip inside the bathroom and allow my body to adjust to the feeling of standing again. Holding on to the sink for support I look at myself in the mirror. I don't recognise the person staring back at me. My hair is dishevelled and matted. There is a huge bruise on my face and my lip is swollen with a cut above it. Looking down I can see bruises on my wrists and my fingernails are dirty and ragged. I sink down on to the toilet and remember what I went through. Nathan was unrecognisable from the man that I had fallen in love with. I know that Ben had warned me about him but I would never have thought that he was as evil as he really was.

Once I have finished I leave the bathroom. As soon as I open the door Ben rushes over to help me. I smile at him and joke, "You never told me I look like I've done

10 rounds in the boxing ring." Ben's expression is grim. "It's no joke Bella. What he has done to you makes me want to do worse to him. For his sake I hope that they don't give me the opportunity." Reaching up I stroke his face. "Let it go Ben. My body will heal and we will forget about him. It could have been a lot worse, let's just be thankful for that." Before he can answer the door opens again and another lady brings a cup of tea into the room. Cheerily she says, "I thought you could use this. I have one for you too if you want it?" she says, beaming over at Ben. Smiling at her he says, "Thank you, that is kind of you." Flushing she says, "Oh it's no trouble, really it isn't." Flustered she leaves the room and we grin at each other. "You haven't lost your touch Ben," I say laughing at him and then all other thoughts leave us as we just enjoy the fact that we are back together again.

Chapter 37

A few days have passed and I am now back at home with Ben. I was discharged later on the same day and Ben brought me back home with him. As soon as we got in I had a deep bath and washed my hair. It felt so good to be clean again and I spent the next couple of days in bed. Ben fussed over me like a mother hen and I wasn't allowed to do anything. He had kept everything that had happened from my parents and Phoebe and Boris and I didn't mention anything when I spoke to them on the phone. I just said that I had resolved everything with Ben and I would catch up with them soon. It wouldn't be long before they knew the whole truth anyway, so a few extra days of pretence wouldn't matter.

It has been such a relief to be back with Ben. He had wanted to sleep in the spare room but I wouldn't let him. I just wanted to feel him close to me again and have enjoyed the feeling of security as I cuddle up to him at night. Other than that he has kept his distance, allowing me to make a full recovery. The need for him is overwhelming but he won't budge on the issue. It's been torture for us both but I can wait a few more days if I have to, after all we have the rest of our lives together.

I still haven't returned to work. Ben won't allow me to go back until I am fully recovered; goodness knows what state I will find it all in when I return. I feel so removed from my old life. The last three weeks have been surreal and I am looking forward to getting back to normality.

Ben and I are sitting watching television when the doorbell rings. Looking over to him I say, "Are you expecting anyone?" Shaking his head he says, "No, not that I'm aware of. Wait here and I'll see who it is." Soon I hear voices in the hallway and then Ben returns, closely followed by the woman I met at the awards dinner, who I now know to be Ben's boss. As I stand she says, "Don't stand up Bella, just stay where you are." She comes over and sits down in the seat opposite me. Turning to Ben she says, "Aren't you going to offer me a drink Ben? I could really do with one." Nodding he leaves to rustle up some drinks and I find myself alone with her again. Smiling at me she says softly, "Now that I've got rid of him I just want to take the opportunity to thank you Bella. I know that I asked a lot of you and it wasn't easy. Ben has well and truly put me in my place over my methods but I think he has forgiven me now." She grins ruefully and once again lowers her voice as she speaks. "Ben is a good operative and I don't want to lose him. However I know that his priorities have changed over the last few months and it worries me. Ordinarily we don't have relationships. They get in the way of our jobs and confuse the matter. Ben has already told me that he wants to take a step back. Understandable I know, but I just want to say before he returns that I don't want to

lose him. I am sure that we can work something out which suits us all and I hope that you will help me out in convincing him to at least try to carry on."
I feel shocked at hearing what she has to say. I never even thought for one minute that Ben was thinking about walking away from his job with the government. However thinking about it I realise that his job is not like most peoples. Before I can answer Ben returns with a tray of coffee and looks between us, his expression wary. His boss says, "Don't look so worried Ben, I was merely thanking Bella for her assistance. Anyway, I have come to update you both on the situation." Handing out the coffees Ben then sits beside me. We look at his boss with interest. This is the first time that we have had any information about the events that unfolded after I was found and curiosity is getting the better of us. His boss carries on. "I just wanted to tell you both that Nathan Matthews and Bradley Summers have been apprehended and are currently in custody in a secure location." I know that the news is not unexpected but it is still a huge shock to hear it. Ben reaches over and squeezes my hand reassuringly. Interrupting her I say, "What about Tina and Melissa, are they also in custody?" I notice a look pass between Ben and his boss and then she nods saying, "You may as well know Bella, but before I say anything you must promise to keep everything I tell you strictly between the three of us. It is very important that you do so for everyone's safety." They both look at me and nodding I say, "Of course I will, you can rely on me." Looking

carefully at me Ben's boss carries on. "Melissa and Tina are also my operatives and Ben's colleagues." The shock is overwhelming and I look between the two of them in disbelief.

"I can't believe it. But Tina is Bradley's girlfriend and has been for years, what do you mean?" Ben looks at his boss and then says gently, "Tina has been working on this for two and a half years. She was deployed to be our man on the inside and get us the information that we needed. She has done a fantastic job and it hasn't been easy for her. This has been her operation and we have all been there to back her up. Melissa became involved when I asked her to help me personally to get you away from Nathan." Snatching my hand away I look between the two of them. Shocked I say, "So it was true. This has all been a big pretence." My head is spinning and I once again realise that my life has been built on a lie. Quickly I stand up. I need to get out of here, it is all too much. Ben jumps up and grabs me spinning me around to face him. "Hear us out Bella; you must know the whole truth. You will see that my actions were not part of the plan. As soon as I realised who your boyfriend was things changed. I risked the whole operation to get you away from him. I couldn't risk you getting involved because I love you and wanted to protect you. Yes Melissa was a lie, but I needed to get you away from him. I would do it again if I had to. I just want you to know that I haven't lied when I say that I love you. Nothing else matters to me but you. Tina was very angry when she realised that I had put a spanner in the works. It was soon obvious that you were an integral part of their plan. They tried everything to get you away from me but nothing worked."

"That was when I had to step in." Ben's boss says. "It became apparent that Ben wouldn't allow you back into Nathan's life so we had to send Melissa in to do the job for us. As luck would have it we didn't realise just how good at it she had been. Nathan had fallen for her, or should I say the person that he thought she was, all engineered to seduce him in the first place. Melissa then became more involved than was first planned. Nathan took her into his confidence and so we were able to use their relationship to engineer their downfall."

Sitting back down I try to digest the information. I can see Ben looking at me anxiously and his boss is merely looking at me with interest. "Are you ok Bella?" Ben asks me with a worried look on his face. "I know this must be a lot to take in and you haven't fully recovered yet from your ordeal." Shakily I smile and say, "I'm ok. Carry on." Ben's boss continues. "All was progressing nicely. The plan was that when Nathan had the codes he would input them and then we would have the proof we needed. We had already put things in place to limit the damage it would cause. Melissa was to take them to an airfield, supposedly to get a flight to France where they would take a connecting flight to Columbia. Tina would be on hand to guarantee your safety and if you were threatened in any way she would step in. We hadn't bargained on

Bradley getting ill and them not making it to the lodge. We also hadn't allowed for the fact that Nathan would discover your duplicity and turn the tables on us by feeding you the sleeping drug and disposing of our monitoring equipment. Once we found out you were compromised we sent Tina in, as it turned out just in the nick of time. She salvaged the operation and engineered your get away."

I notice that Ben's expression is grim and he has turned ashen. He says, "Tina went back to the lodge and told Nathan that you had attacked her and run away. He was angry and blamed her but luckily Bradley stepped in and prevented him from attacking her. He took off to find you but luckily as it was dark he was unsuccessful. Melissa meanwhile turned up and he returned. They all left and then myself and the search party took over to look for you. The rest you know."

Ben's boss takes up the story. "They drove to the airfield and boarded the helicopter. Nathan used the laptop that he bought for you to enter the last codes. The plan was that once they were entered correctly it would start a chain of events that would empty the accounts of every contact that they had stored up over the last three years, including several big businesses. The money would be transferred into an offshore bank account opened in your name Bella. Nathan had control of the account but all traces would lead back to you. The account was in your name, the computer used was in your name and everything that Nathan has bought over the last year is in your name. The notebook was used so that once again it would point to your guilt. Nothing leads to him." As I listen to her relay the story, the full enormity of what Nathan was planning begins to hit me. He wasn't kidding when he said that I was to be the fall guy. Luckily for me he was found out long before his plan could take effect. Thinking about Tina and all that she must have gone through makes my blood run cold. As I look at the two of them I wonder what world it is that they all live in. To put your own life on hold for the sake of an operation is alien to me. Looking over at Ben I wonder what he has also had to do in the line of duty. It doesn't bear thinking about and I push the thoughts firmly from my mind. I can see them both watching me and I say shakily, "What happens now? I mean I must be implicated in all of this. Do I have to make a statement or go anywhere?" Ben's boss shakes her head. "Not at the moment. You will be required to make a statement soon but there is no rush. We have to deal with Nathan and Bradley first. Because of the insider knowledge and evidence gained from our surveillance your statement will just be the final nail in the coffin." "But what about Tina. Won't they realise that she has set them up and also blame her for some of it." Ben says, "Tina is long gone. As far as they will know, both her and Melissa got away, possibly to Columbia as arranged. They will both disappear without a trace. There will be no evidence linking them to any crime so they are no longer needed."

There is so much to take in and process. Everything is spinning around in my mind and as I think of a question another one takes its place. Ben's boss stands up. "Anyway, I must go. I just wanted to let you both know the current position. You must have a lot to talk about. We will be in touch but try to put it all behind you for now and come to terms with it all." Holding out her hand she shakes mine saying, "Thank you again Bella. We may make an operative of you yet." Ben scowls at her and says, "Not if I have anything to do with it you won't." She laughs and says, "Walk with me to the door Ben. I need a word." As I watch them go I wonder what she has to say to him. Sitting back down I go over everything that I have learned. I still can't take it all in and I know that it will be some

time before I can. Ben soon returns with a grim expression on his face. I look up at him questioningly and shrugging his shoulders he says, "I told her that I have had enough. I told her the day you left. I would only stay on until you were safe and then I was done. She tried to change my mind, but it is done. I can't go back to that life." Going over to him I draw him close to me. He looks at me with surprise. "You must hate me Bella. You can see what sort of world I operate in. Everything is manipulated to achieve whatever I want it to. Please believe me though when I say that I never intended to manipulate you. When I found you again my only goal was to save you from Nathan. Of course I wanted you, I always have, but if you had not wanted me then I would have walked away." I put my finger to his lips to silence him. "Enough Ben. I cannot believe what lengths you have gone to to protect me. How on earth could I be angry at that? You saved me and I love you more now than I thought I did before. The fact that you want to give up your life for me, it is too much to think about." Ben's eyes soften as he looks down at me. "No Bella, it is you who have saved me. I was lost before I found you again. Now I have I see a future for us both. I don't want to operate in the shadows anymore. I want a normal life and that is why I started to buy up the stores, long before I found you again. This change has been planned for some time now; the fact that I now have you in my life makes it all the sweeter."

Quickly I pull him towards me and kiss him deeply. Pulling back I say, "For goodness sake Ben, stop talking. All of this can wait. Please just take me to bed I have waited long enough." Ben looks at me with such love which quickly changes to one of potent desire. Huskily he says, "I thought you'd never ask."

Epilogue

TWO WEEKS LATER

Today Ben and I are helping Phoebe and Boris move into their new home. The last couple of weeks have been a whirlwind. The news soon broke about Nathan and Bradley. My parents were so shocked. They heard about it from Nathan's Mum who is devastated. My parents had also been equally devastated. It took them some time for it all to sink in. We all trusted Nathan and to learn that he had been planning to rob millions of people and businesses was almost too much to take in. My parents were glad that I had not been involved and much to my amusement changed their opinions overnight. In their minds Ben is my knight in shining armour. He rescued me from the evil villain, although this is all in their imagination as I haven't been able to tell them anything of Ben's involvement in all of this. I am just glad that they are happy for me and have accepted Ben as my boyfriend once and for all. I felt sorry for Nathan's family though as they are good people. I can't begin to understand what they are going through and just hope that they can soon come to terms with it all. I made my statement, which was as stated just a formality. I will be required to testify if it goes to trial, which will only happen if they plead

-not guilty.
I returned to work last week and was grateful to get back to what I know and love. April was very pleased to see me. She had done a brilliant job covering for me whilst I was away and I told Ben that when the opportunity presented itself she should be promoted. He had laughed and said that she could have my job as he wanted me to work with him at Head Office. I declined the offer, living with him is one thing but

working together would be impossible.
I love our life together. Ben is now much more relaxed and less busy than he was. We spend most of our time like any other couple would. We have friends and a social life and enjoy spending time around the house at the weekends. He is as intense as always in the bedroom which I am not complaining about.

Phoebe and Boris are now moving in to the neighbouring village and I can't wait. I hear Ben calling me and soon we are on our way to their new house to help them move in. "I thought this day would never come," I say to Ben as we head off. He nods, "Yes, it seems a lifetime ago that they asked us. A lot has happened since."
"Yes it certainly has. Let's hope that life is uneventful from now on." He smiles and I am pleased to see how happy he looks. As we pull in to their drive I can see several large removal Lorries are already here. Phoebe is directing them all in brandishing her usual clip board. As she sees us a smile breaks out over her face,

"Bella, Ben, welcome to our new home." We hug her and she says, "Ben, Boris is inside you can ask him what help he needs. Bella, would you start unpacking the boxes in the kitchen? As soon as you find a kettle and supplies could you make everyone a drink? This lot only run on Tea and they must be nearing empty by now." I hear a nearby removal man laugh. "She's not wrong." He says, "Oh and don't forget the biscuits love, they help a lot with our energy levels." I grin at Phoebe and follow the man inside, leaving her to carry on directing.

I had forgotten how lovely their new home is. They will be so happy here. Phoebe is a country girl at heart and I can see that they will soon have a menagerie of animals to care for, and I doubt it will be long before they start a family. I am glad they are settled. I love them both very much and am ecstatic that they will be living so close by.

I can see Boris chatting to Ben in a large room that must be the living room. Any awkwardness between them is long gone. Boris has grown to love Ben as much as I do and is grateful for his friendship. I couldn't be happier than I am at this moment. Suddenly Ben catches my eye. A broad smile breaks out across his face and the love that I feel for him threatens to overwhelm me. Finally the jigsaw is complete. I am happier than I have ever been in my life, we found each other again, we were always meant to be together and now we were and now nothing can come between us.

THE END

Thank you for reading The Matter Of Trust.
I hope that you enjoyed it as much as I did writing it.
If you have please look out for my other books:
The story will continue in,
Payback.

You can also find me on Face book - S J Crabb Book Information page, you can also follow me on Twitter: SJCrabb@Crabb1SJ - where I will post details of any future releases. I would welcome any feedback and look forward to hearing from you.

From time to time I offer my books free on promotion. If you would like to receive information about any promotions, offers or New Releases please e mail me on: scrabbauthor@gmail.com

I do not share any information with other parties.

The Diary Of Madison Brown

Premier Deception

The One That Got Away
(Part One of The Hardcastle Saga)

Payback
(Part Three of The Hardcastle Saga)

Payback

By

S J Crabb

Prologue

Vanessa closed the magazine that she had been reading. The advert had caught her attention and reminded her of some unfinished business.
She thought back two years ago. How different her life had been then. She was married to a self obsessed brute of a man who had been lined up as her husband for as long as she could remember. Her family had thought that it had been the perfect match. The marriage would unite the two dynasties and ensure its longevity. They hadn't realised what a truly abhorrent creature he really was. Surely if they had they would never have given the union their seal of approval. I say union rather than marriage because it was more like a dictatorship. Claude had been the most hideous, reprehensible, disgusting human being that Vanessa had ever had the misfortune to come across, and she had married him. It hadn't been that obvious at first, probably because he was on his best behaviour. However it soon became obvious that he had only married her for her inheritance and her bloodline. Being the daughter of a Lord and a well respected business man had many advantages to somebody keen to elevate himself up the social ladder. She in turn had been dazzled by him. He well and truly swept her off her feet.

The courtship hadn't been long. She fell for him hook, line and sinker and they were married shortly afterwards. The wedding had been the society event of the year if not the decade. The guest list was a veritable Who's Who and it was a marriage made in heaven. If only she had known then what she grew to know, she would have realised that it was not Heaven but one made in Hell. As time went on she began to realise the type of person that she had married. He soon started to bully her, both emotionally and physically. Any thoughts or suggestions that she had he shouted down. He belittled her opinions and made her out to be stupid and vacuous to his friends. In company he played the attentive husband but in private he ridiculed her and dented her confidence. He was always harsh in his criticism of her appearance and enjoyed comparing her unfavourably with their friend's wives. He called her dowdy and unattractive and declared her physically repulsive to him. Their sex life had never been good and he merely went through the motions to produce an heir. The fact that they hadn't managed it fuelled his anger and he blamed her for being barren. Vanessa however had thought it a blessing in disguise as the last thing she wanted was to bring a replica of him into the world.

Before long he started a series of affairs. He was very indiscreet about it and enjoyed taunting her with his exploits. He moved into his own room and even began to bring his conquests home. Soon she became a laughing stock. She lost her friends and her family blamed her for not being able to hold on to her man.

Her own self confidence hit rock bottom. She even hated herself. They couldn't all be wrong. It must have been true what he said.

Soon she believed everything he told her and one day she decided to end it all. Unfortunately for her she was found before it was too late. She had taken a cocktail of drugs, intending never to wake up. Her maid found her and raised the alarm.

She had then spent several months in an institution on suicide watch at the request of her "loving" husband. He had played a blinder. Everyone felt so much sympathy for him. He had tried to be a good husband but she had become unbalanced and needy. He told everyone that she had turned to drink, even though she never touched a drop. He lamented her downfall in public and celebrated it in private. Despite her incarceration she was actually quite glad to be free from him. Life at the institution became her saviour. It was her sanctuary and she could finally live without the fear of him. He never visited, telling everyone that asked that he couldn't bear to see what she had become. It suited her well. He was the last person she wanted to see anyway.

Sadly her new found life was to be short lived. Her father died and she was his sole heir. She would inherit his fortune and title and so it was with a great deal of publicity that she was deemed cured of her depression and re united with her loving husband. He

in turn would take her father's place as Chairman of the bank and she would resume her role as his loving wife. What she didn't realise at the time was that she had the power to divorce her despicable husband. Because she was in such a fragile mental state she just accepted everything that he told her.

Life carried on as before and she threw herself into social engagements and headed up various charities. Anything to escape from her loneliness and empty marriage. Claude was wrapped up with life at the bank and she was wheeled out only when he needed her beside him at the various functions and social engagements. Their marriage became one of convenience. They existed together as virtual strangers in private and a loving couple in public. However it soon became apparent that her husband was not as good a business man as her father had been. Stories began to reach her about his bad management and dodgy dealings. He became increasingly difficult to live with and once again blamed her for his problems. Things were spiralling out of control until one day he appointed somebody new to the Bank. That man became his saviour and also much to her surprise hers. That man was Ben Hardcastle. He took over the everyday running of the bank, freeing Claude up from making any decisions of any importance. When they met at social functions she found herself drawn to him. He was extremely attractive and good company. They struck up an unlikely friendship and she began to very much look forward to seeing him again. She started to think of reasons to visit the bank and engineered many supposed chance meetings with him. Soon she became obsessed with him. He was everything her husband wasn't.

Their relationship changed following an extremely dull charity event. Claude had reverted back to his philandering ways and was extremely indiscreet about it. At the dinner it was obvious that his latest conquest was also invited and he spent most of the evening with her. Vanessa was once again being publicly ridiculed and was the subject of a lot of gossip amongst the diners. Ben had noticed the situation and heard the rumours. He spent the evening keeping her company. That in itself wasn't surprising, after all she was his boss's wife and they were seated at the same table. As the evening progressed they discovered that they had many things in common. She enjoyed his company and as it appeared, he enjoyed hers. When he asked her to dance she jumped at the chance, and when he took her in his arms she experienced feelings that she never had before. She longed for him to hold her close and his close proximity was sending alien feelings of longing and desire through her. Much to her surprise he appeared to feel the same. Claude had disappeared with his latest conquest which was no surprise to her. Noticing that she was alone Ben has whispered to her, inviting her to his room for a nightcap. She had not hesitated and had followed him to his room, after a discreet interval so as not to set tongues wagging. That night had been the best night of her life. Ben had taken her to places that she never knew existed. Never before had she experienced such feelings. Their lovemaking was intense and had carried on long into the night. She never wanted the evening to end and when it did she cried with the desolation that she felt on leaving him. Thus began a secret affair that re invented her. She felt desired and loved and truly blossomed as a person. She was in love and it was obvious for all to see. Even Claude began to notice that she had changed. She was more confident and had began to take more care in her appearance. She went out a lot more and had developed a wicked sense of humour. She had blossomed into a beautiful desirable woman and obviously no longer needed him.

Then it all changed. Claude saw her in a new light. He began to stay home a lot more. He demanded more of her time and started to make advances towards her sexually. They hadn't slept together for many years and the more she resisted him the more he tried. Through all of this she was seeing Ben. They met as often as possible, which wasn't often enough as far as she was concerned. She could cope with her repulsive husband's advances as long as she had Ben in her life. It wasn't long though before Claude grew impatient. The fact that she spurned him only made him want her more. One evening before she was due to meet Ben in secret, Claude struck. She was ready to go out and it soon became obvious that her husband had had too much to drink. He was waiting for her in the hallway. Blocking her exit he told her to stay with him that evening. They had a terrible argument and he struck her across the face. Pulling her into the drawing room he had then proceeded to physically assault her. She was no match for him and his attack lasted long into the night. There was nobody to save her as he had given the servants the night off. He raped her several times and beat her black and blue. By the time he had finished she was a quivering wreck and once again he had destroyed her.

The attack set her back years. Claude carried on as normal, offering her no apology, just telling her that she needed to be put in her place. She was his wife and her obligation was to him. She secreted herself in her room and didn't come out for days.

It must have been three days later that Ben came to the house. Claude had left and he came on the pretence of delivering some documents for Claude to sign. As soon as she saw him she broke down. He had been shocked and appalled and urged her to leave with him. She had been so tempted but during her time in her room she had had time to think. Despite her beating and mental torture she was no longer the woman she once was. Ben had shown her another way and a plan had begun to form in her mind.

As she remembered what happened next Vanessa smiled to herself. Ben Hardcastle had saved her not only once but twice. Without him she could never have carried out what happened next. Now as she looked at the advertisement she realised that she needed his help again. This time though he wouldn't know it but he would be saving himself too. It was time to get back in touch.

Coming soon in 2016

Email me at:
scrabbauthor@gmail.com for information on its release.

Printed in Great Britain
by Amazon